TOXIC AF

BEY DECKARD

CONTENTS

THEMES & CONTENT WARNINGS

This story contains: rape, coercion, blackmail, abuse, abuse of power/power imbalance, toxic relationship, resource control (food, money), CNC, dubcon/noncon, humiliation/degradation, public sex, PTSD, anxiety, crying, weight loss due to stress, face slapping, physical violence between MCs, threat and terror, injury, hospitalization, surgery, unsafe sex, fisting/forced fisting & gaping, choking, stalking, voyeurism, mild feminization, lingerie, sadomasochism, DP, gangbang, spanking, references to past child abuse, internalized homophobia/homophobia, and homophobic language.

It's not a pretty story.

AUTHOR'S NOTE

This book is written in Canadian English.
This means it's colo*u*r, not color; analy*z*e, not analyse, gr*e*y, not gray; cent*re*, not center; and label*l*ing, not labeling, etc.

More on Canadian English:
https://en.wikipedia.org/wiki/Canadian_English#Spelling
(If you're curious)

Also . . . Yes, I know Montreal cops don't wear peaked cop hats on duty. They wear caps. But I wanted Mitch in a peaked cap because I really like Kake by Tom of Finland.

PS - I added a lexicon at the back in case you run into unfamiliar terms

SOUNDTRACK

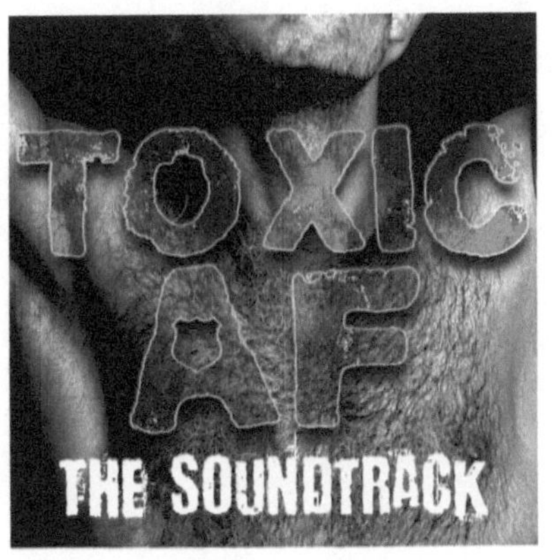

http://geni.us/ToxicAFOST

CHAPTER 1
CRUISING

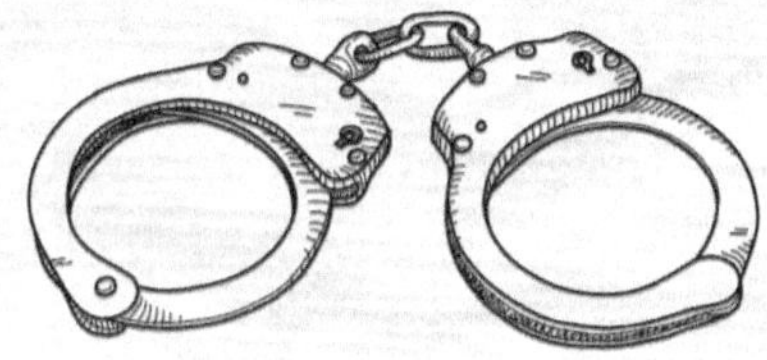

JULY

The sun was just setting as I strolled along one of Parc Angrignon's many winding paths, heading toward my favourite secluded bench. I was in *such* a great mood. I'd spent all afternoon just chilling and playing video games, and I was about to get some anonymous dick—an absolutely *perfect* way to end the day. I smiled and slipped my hand down my shorts, squeezing my boner as my excitement made me walk a little faster. I left the path to take a shortcut through the cedar bushes and nearly bumped into two guys fucking behind it.

I smiled and apologized as I skirted around them, then went down the slope to the bench. Sometimes, I had to wait a bit because someone else was using it, but when I cleared the little stand of trees, I saw the bench was free. *Sweet.*

Grinning, I undid my shorts and sat down, my dick standing up stiff and straight from my lap, and started stroking myself slowly, waiting in anticipation for someone to join me.

I didn't have long to wait. An older guy spotted me from the small lakeside path and approached with one hand down the front of his pants. He stood there watching me play with myself for a little while as he jerked off, but when he made no move to approach, I let my shorts slide all the way off so that I could put my heels up on the bench and show him my hole. That did the trick. The old guy exhaled hard and stepped up to me, taking my cock in hand while I reached up to undo his pants. His cock was a nice size, but he wasn't hard enough yet, so I jerked him off until he was.

"I can fuck you?" he murmured in French.

I nodded and reached into the pocket of my hoodie for a condom. I handed it to him, and while he put it on, I grabbed the bottle of lube from my shorts and turned around to kneel on the bench. Using my fingers, I pushed a little bit of lube into my hole, then waited.

The guy was so eager to fuck me that he went in too fast and deep, and I grunted in pain, pushing him back.

"Hey, watch it," I said, holding him in place for a few seconds until my hole relaxed. "Okay, now go." I released him and braced myself on the bench's backrest.

The guy started fucking me slowly, obviously being careful not to hurt me again, but when I started pushing back into him eagerly, he got the message and began thrusting quickly.

"Oh fuck," I whispered. "Yeah . . . Daddy, give it to me." My boner was swinging around between my legs as the old guy ploughed my hole, but I didn't want to touch myself *just* yet. I was already feeling so good that I was afraid I'd cum too soon. I'd save it for the next guy that came along. Or maybe the guy after that.

I could tell the old guy was getting close by how hard he was breathing. He was so loud that I hadn't realized we'd been joined by someone else until a hand closed around my cock. I turned with a gasp and saw the man fondling my dick was a chubby, balding guy with a big moustache. I smiled at him as I moved his hand from my dick up to my chest, and he happily obliged me by playing with my nipples while he waited for his turn at my ass.

The old guy let out a quiet, guttural moan as he gave me a few hard thrusts, shaking so hard as he came that I was worried he'd have a heart attack. But then he let out a raspy chuckle and pulled out, sitting next to me on the bench to recover with the cum-filled tip of the condom drooping down the side of his shaft as he sat there panting.

I handed another condom to Mr. Moustache as the gravel crunched behind me, announcing that we'd been joined by a third and then, a few moments later, a fourth.

Wow. Sure, I'd be sore tomorrow, but I was thrilled by how the evening was turning out.

The second guy didn't last very long at all, and I was *just* starting to edge myself with the third guy's cock deep in my guts when I heard a fifth guy approaching. But then a flashlight clicked on, and the beam swept over the bench, blinding me. *Shit.* The guy fucking me pulled out with a shout, and I fell backwards off the bench in my hurry to grab my shorts, landing on my side with a grunt as the group scattered. Wincing in pain and terrified, I shielded my eyes as the big black boots approached.

"Please . . . I've never done anything like this before," I said in French to the cop standing over me.

"I doubt that very much," he replied in English. He cocked his head, then took off his hat and squatted next to me, staring at me hard. He had a face like a comic book hero—square-jawed and so chiselled and ridiculously handsome with dark brows over pale eyes that I momentarily forgot that I was in trouble. *And* that I hate cops.

"What am I going to do with you?" he asked softly, flaring his nostrils.

"You're going to let me go because you're a really nice guy?" I chuckled nervously.

"Nah. Don't think so." As he stood, he hauled me up by my bicep, then shoved me back towards the bench.

I stumbled but caught myself, my heart pounding so hard it

was difficult to breathe as I sat there staring up at him, my bare ass cold on the wooden bench.

The cop tossed his hat down beside me, then reached for his fly.

"What's going on?" I whispered though I had a good idea what his intentions were when he pulled out his dick.

"Well, young man, first you're going to suck my cock, and then I'm gonna fuck you with it."

Suddenly, I didn't find him handsome anymore.

I let out a shuddering breath. What could I do? Scream for help? What good would that do? He was a fucking cop, and cops got away with everything. I was a fucking nobody. A loser with a crappy job and piles of student debt.

I sighed and nodded, reaching for his dick as he stepped up to me.

Holy shit. I stared at his cock as it swelled in my hands. It wasn't long, but it was fucking *thick.* I licked my lips uneasily and cleared my throat, wondering how the hell I was going to fit something the size of a pop can in my mouth.

"Come on, cocksucker," the cop growled, grabbing the back of my head to mash my face into his dick. "And if I feel teeth, I'm going to break your fucking nose."

I whimpered, tears blurring my vision. "Okay. Okay." I opened wide, terrified of grazing him with my teeth, and started blowing him. Obviously unsatisfied with the little I could fit in my mouth, he held onto my head and began forcing his dick in deeper. I started choking and pushed at him in a panic, which only made him laugh.

I managed to jerk my head free and coughed as drool and tears dripped off my chin, but he yanked me by the hair and forced his fat cock back into my mouth.

"Jesus, you're pathetic," he said, sounding frustrated as he gave up trying to choke me with his dick. I gagged as his cock came free, and I sat there gasping and gulping for air as I sobbed.

"Please," I rasped.

"Do you want me to drag you to the station? I've got you on public indecency . . . Solicitation," he said, counting off on his fingers. "Resisting arrest . . . hmm, what else could I tack on?"

I just stared at him, my heart in my throat. Solicitation? Resisting arrest? *What?* I felt like I was in a nightmare.

"So, what is it going to be, son?"

My bottom lip wobbled as the tears leaked down my cheeks. Nothing in his expression gave me hope that he'd be gentle with me.

"Okay," I whispered pathetically.

"Turn around and spread those cheeks."

I scrabbled in my pocket for a condom and held it out to him with a shaking hand, but he just batted it away with a sneer.

I knew there was no point in arguing, so I turned around like he asked and was actually surprised that he waited until I'd lubed up before positioning himself behind me. As he began pushing his massive cock against my hole, I let out a ragged sob, so terrified that I was trembling like a leaf. No amount of lube in the world would make this any better for me. I'd never had something so big in my ass before, and even if he *was* being gentle, which he wasn't, it was going to hurt.

As his cockhead began stretching me open, I panted, then when I couldn't hold back my whimpers of pain, he punched me in the back of the head before putting his hand around my mouth to stifle my cries. It felt like being split open—an excruciating, gut-clenching pain that made my vision swim. I went limp as he began fucking me, driving himself deeper until his whole dick was forced into me with one hard thrust, and I screamed against his palm. For a moment, I thought I would black out, which would have been a mercy . . . but no, I was fully conscious as I waited for the cop to finish raping me.

It might only have been a few minutes, but it felt like an eternity. I knew there would be blood. I'd probably need to go to the hospital. I groaned, my eyes clenched shut, praying for it to be over.

And then it was. The cop came with a few low grunts and body-jarring thrusts and stayed put to fill my ravaged insides with his disgusting rapist cum. When he finally pulled out, I just sagged over the back of the bench, weeping quietly.

"There. That wasn't so bad, was it?" the cop said, tucking himself away in his pants.

I turned to stare at him through my tears. My breath kept hitching in my chest as I rasped out, "W-w-will you take me to the hosp-p-pital?"

The cop scoffed. "The hospital? Why d'you want to go to the hospital? You're fine."

"I'm blee—" A sob broke through as I struggled to get the words out. "I'm bleeding."

"Bleeding?" He took his flashlight out of his belt and clicked it on, shining it on my ass for a second. "You might walk bowlegged for a while, but you're not *bleeding*. Jesus."

"I'm not?" I timidly reached back to touch myself, and my fingers came away wet, but sure enough, it was just cum and lube. I grimaced and wiped my hand on the bench, turning around to sit gingerly.

The cop picked my shorts off the grass, but instead of passing them to me, he rifled my pockets and took out my wallet.

"You're not satisfied with just raping me, so now you're going to rob me?" I said, drying my cheeks with the sleeve of my hoodie.

"You're funny." He snorted a laugh. "No . . . I'm just taking note of this." He held up my driver's licence, then took his phone out to take a picture of the front and back of the card. "There. Now I know where to find you . . ." He squinted at the small lettering. "Patrick Bouchard."

"Why?" I blinked at him in alarm, my heart racing.

He put my card back in my wallet and tossed the wallet in my lap. Then he picked up his hat and put it back on, adjusting it as he smiled at me. "Because your ass belongs to me now. See?" He pulled out his phone again, tapped at it, then turned it towards me.

My mouth went dry. Before making his presence known, the cop had stood there filming me for several minutes. The video was dark, but not so much that you couldn't tell it was me getting ploughed in a park.

"Now I know your name and where you live. I can easily find out who your boss is. Or your parents. Do you think they'd be interested to know about your little predilection for getting your ass drilled in public?"

"So it's blackmail then."

"Sure is." He chuckled, then turned away. "Be seeing you around."

I realized then that I didn't even know his name.

CHAPTER 2
THE WAIT

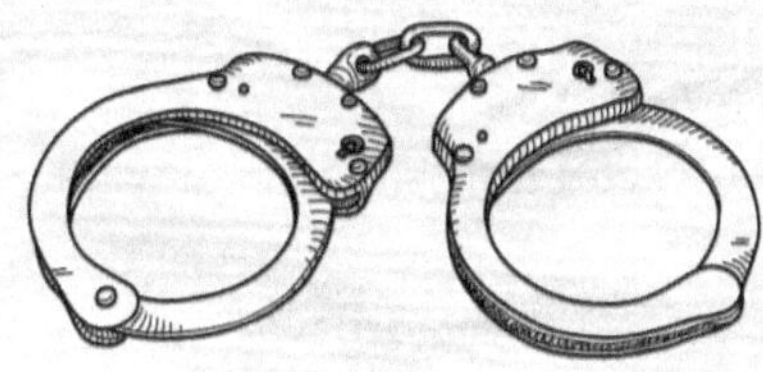

My ass was tender for a while, but as that got better, my nerves got worse. I lived in terror. Whenever I saw a police cruiser pass my apartment, I was sure it was him. Every knock on the door would send me into a panic. I couldn't leave my house. I couldn't sleep. I couldn't even shower for more than a minute at a time because what if he somehow snuck in while I couldn't hear? In just a week, I'd lost five pounds—which I couldn't really afford to lose—and was on the verge of losing my job.

Was the cop serious about coming for me? Was he just fucking with me? In a daze, I wandered my apartment, checking the windows and checking the locks on the door. Over and over and over again. I was making myself sick. *Maybe this is just a mind game. Maybe he'll never come. Maybe he's watching me right now . . .* I stopped in front of the window and twitched aside the curtain to scan the street.

"Where are you, you fucker?" I whispered. It was the not knowing that was the worst. At least if I *knew* he was coming, I could prepare myself. I could steel my nerves.

"Fuck." I knuckled my eyes, absolutely exhausted. "*Fuck.*"

I hated him. I hated what he had done to me. I hated what he was doing to me now.

. . .

Feeling as skittish as a deer, I stood on the front stoop of my apartment, breathing slowly and deeply to calm my nerves. I *had* to go to work. If I missed one more shift, my boss would have no choice but to can me.

Patrick . . . you can do this.

I clenched my fists and took the stairs down to the sidewalk.

So far, so good.

The little grocery store where I worked was only three blocks away. I could sprint there in less than a minute. Then I'd be . . . what? Safe? Safer than being alone in my apartment, yes.

I squared my shoulders.

Let's do this.

My shift passed quickly, and I was starting to feel pretty good by the end of it. I was even joking around and gossiping with Khadim and Maude like usual. All in all, I was starting to feel . . . normal.

And that's why it was such a punch in the gut when I looked over to see who the next customer was, and it was *him*.

The scanning gun fell out of my hand and swung back and forth on its stretched-out spiralled wire as I stared at the cop in shock. He was out of uniform and wore a baseball cap, but I would have recognized him instantly, no matter what he wore. He smiled pleasantly at me. In the light of day, I could see that his eyes were a pale, icy blue and that he had a sprinkling of grey in the black hair at his temples.

"Patrick."

I swallowed. "S-sir. Officer." I felt like I was going to be sick.

"Please. Call me Mitch."

"Mitch," I repeated faintly.

He continued to smile at me, but after a few moments, he

raised his eyebrows and wrinkled his brow expectantly. "Uh . . . my groceries."

"Yes. Groceries." I clutched the counter so I wouldn't fall over as I fumbled for the scanner and forced myself to breathe around the giant ball of terror in my chest. I quickly scanned his items—a block of cheese, deodorant, a bag of apples—then froze when I saw the bottle of lube.

"I thought I might drop by for a visit," Mitch said with a grin, pushing the lube closer to me so I could scan it. "You're nearly done, right?"

I lifted my eyes and stared at him, wishing I could scream or call for help. But he had that video of me, and the thought of him showing it to my parents was more than I could bear.

"I'll meet you outside. I know it's just a few blocks to your place, but I'll give you a lift. Sound good?"

Numbly, I handed him his receipt and nodded, then watched him leave.

"Oh my god," Maude said, leaning over the partition with a wide grin, completely oblivious to my panic. "Who was *that*?"

"Um. Just someone I know," I said quietly. *The man who raped me and who is planning on raping me again today.*

"He is *hot*. Oh, those *eyes*," she said, fanning herself. "I'd *definitely* call him Daddy."

I turned away so she wouldn't see the tears in my eyes and began closing out my cash.

"What did I miss?" Khadim asked, pushing a line of stacked carts.

"I think Pat has a new boyfriend."

I fumbled the roll of dimes, dropping it back into the tray. Spots swam in my vision. "Watch my cash," I rasped as I hopped over the counter, bolting for the bathroom. I barely made it to the toilet before hurling my guts out.

. . .

My hands were shaking so badly that it took three tries to get the key into the lock, and then when I went to turn it, I ended up yanking the key out.

"*Jesus* . . . give it here." Mitch took the key from me, unlocked my front door, and held it open so I could go in first. I walked like a zombie to the middle of my living room, then flinched at the sound of the lock turning.

"Come here, Patrick."

I hated the confidence in his voice—the total authority in his tone. *Hated* it. Hated him. I turned and, keeping my head down, stepped toward him.

"What's the matter, sunshine?"

I curled my lip and shuddered as Mitch's hand closed around the back of my neck.

"Hey, don't be like that." He squeezed me gently. Then he put his mouth near my ear. "Now, take off your pants like a good boy."

I let out a soft moan, and my eyes filled with tears again. *Would* it be so bad if my mom and dad saw me getting railed by randos?

Yes. Yes, it would be. They'd be mortified. I couldn't do that to them.

I undid my pants and let them and my boxers drop down to puddle around my ankles, then listlessly stepped out of them.

Mitch chuckled, steering me toward the couch so he could bend me over the arm, then proceeded to drip cold lube onto my hole, roughly pushing some into me with his fingers.

"I would have come by sooner," he said conversationally as he fingered my ass some more. "But I had to take care of something to do with work." Seemingly satisfied with the amount of lube he'd put into me, he wiped his fingers on my ass cheek and then immediately started poking at my sphincter with his thick, bullet-shaped dick. "D'you miss me?"

I ignored him, trying to make myself relax, then let out a strangled cry as he suddenly jammed his cock into me.

"Please!" I said through clenched teeth. "Please . . . not so hard. *Please* be careful."

"Careful? You're not made out of porcelain, darlin'. I think we've already proven that your sweet pink hole can take a bit of punishment." He thrust hard, forcing me open so quickly that I screamed.

"I hope your neighbours aren't home," Mitch said with a laugh as he gave my burning, raw hole a few hard thrusts. "Maybe you better keep it down, eh?"

I buried my face in the couch cushion to muffle my cries as he took his time with me, his rock-hard cock like a battering ram in my guts. Soon, I was sobbing so hard I started choking—Mitch let out an annoyed groan and stopped fucking me so he could flip me over onto my back on the couch. He stared down at me for a moment with his pale eyes narrowed, then slapped me hard across the face.

I wailed, my hands covering my stinging cheek as he forced my legs open to ram his dick back into me straight to the balls, getting another scream out of me in the process. He clamped a hand over my mouth, thrusting hard and fast, and I stared into his eyes as he continued to rape me.

Mitch started grunting in time with his thrusts, slowing as his face reddened, then a deep wrinkle appeared between his dark brows and with his gaze locked on mine, he let out a growl, emptying his balls into me as I lay there helplessly pinned beneath him.

He let out a deep sigh and closed his eyes, shivering as he thrust slowly into me a few more times. Then he smiled and moved back, pulling his softening cock out of my hole in the process.

"Will you look at that," he said, shaking his head as he stared down at me. I thought at first he was talking about the ruin of my ass, but when he lightly flicked my cock, I realized that I had an erection.

I felt sick.

"So, you *did* miss me." Mitch laughed, batting my cock back and forth with his index finger. Then he took my hand and put it on my dick before getting up to sit on the armchair across from the couch. "Why don't you put on a little show for me?"

Frowning, I flared my nostrils. "You got what you came for."

"Yeah, I know," he said, lacing his fingers over his belly. Below his T-shirt, his limp cock lay drying. "But this'll be fun. And who knows, maybe watching you blow your load will turn me on, and I can have a second go at you." He shrugged with a crooked grin as he put his feet up on the coffee table, getting comfortable. "Go on. Show me what you got."

I clenched my jaw.

"Let me put it this way: if you refuse, I'll break one of your fingers. Or your nose. Up to you."

Furious tears blurred my vision as I began to jerk myself off, and I was both surprised and ashamed by how little it took to bring myself to orgasm. I let out a cry as the cum erupted out of me in just a matter of minutes, the muscle contractions pulsating the sore tissues of my ass, sharpening my climax. Afterwards, I lay there panting, a big puddle of cum on my chest. I whimpered when Mitch rose up before me, his hand around his reinvigorated cock.

"Round two," he said, smiling down at me.

I moaned and closed my eyes.

CHAPTER 3
CONDITIONED

AUGUST

SOMETIMES, Mitch would call in the middle of the night to make sure I'd be home in case he wanted to use me on the way to work. Other times, he'd call me at the grocery store to let me know that he was in the neighbourhood. He'd have me take breaks so I could run out to meet him at my place, and he'd be balls-deep inside me the minute the door closed. Afterwards, I'd have to quickly walk back to work with my busted hole all swollen and burning with his cum leaking out of me. It was embarrassing—I started stuffing Kleenex down my pants just to save my underwear.

The most shameful part of it all was the Pavlovian reaction I'd developed whenever my phone rang. As soon as it buzzed, my chest would seize up with dread, and then my dick would get hard.

Every. *Single*. Time.

My coworkers noticed something was off with me, so I started keeping to myself. I avoided people in general. I pretty much stopped calling my mom, and when she called me, our conversations lasted only a few minutes before I made excuses. I was too afraid I'd break down on the phone with her and tell her everything.

I lived in terror of Mitch, and *yet* . . . there I was in the bathroom at work several times a week, furiously masturbating just because a telemarketer or a wrong number had called me and set off my dick.

I lost more weight. I would start crying uncontrollably at the drop of a hat. My hands trembled. The bags under my eyes had bags of their own. My left ear wouldn't stop ringing. I threw up at least once a day. My dreams were a carousel of nightmares.

And my ass hurt. All the time.

And *yet* . . .

"Please. *Please* don't." I gasped and struggled as he pressed his cockhead to my pucker. "That's not enough lube. You're going to tear something."

"I like it when I go in a little dry," he murmured in my ear. "Feels good." He bit down on my shoulder and then thrust his dick into me, choking off my squeal of pain by crushing my windpipe in his hand. I writhed beneath him. Already light-headed from the pain, I was now also fighting to breathe as he continued to destroy my ass. Trapped beneath me, my cock was hard and soaking the sheets with precum.

"Fuck yeah," Mitch said with a chuckle as he released my throat. "Tell me to cum in your ass, Patrick."

I shook my head. I hated it when he made me say things.

Growling, Mitch took a handful of my hair and bit me again, and this time, he let me scream.

"Say it. Say you want me to breed your sloppy hole." Mitch took my earlobe between his teeth, and I was so scared he'd bite it right off that I whimpered and nodded.

"Okay! Hang on. Okay, okay . . . I want you . . . to cum in my ass," I said in a trembling voice. "Please," I added, desperate for it to be over.

"Mm. That's right, baby." He panted, and I could feel his dick surge in my chafed hole. "I'm gonna paint your guts with cum." His hand closed around my throat as he began choking me again, chuckling as I tried to fight him off. All my struggling did was make my ass tighten around his cock, which he loved.

He grunted and fucked me quickly as he came, and I closed my eyes, close to passing out from lack of oxygen but relieved that it was almost over.

Finally, he released me, and I attempted to wriggle out from under him, coughing as I tried to catch my breath, but he startled me by pinning me to the mattress by the back of my neck.

"That's the biggest fucking gaping asshole I've ever seen," he said, laughing, and I yelped as he thrust a few fingers into me, swirling them around in his cum. "I wonder if I can stick my whole fist in there."

"No. Oh *god*." I grabbed his wrist, trying to free my neck as he worked another finger into me. I'd gotten to the point where I could take his cock without *too* much pain, but his hands were *huge*. "Please *please* no. It won't fit." I moaned as he stretched my ass with his fingers.

"But I have to *try* . . . don't I?" He paused for a second to add more lube, then went back to rotating his hand, trying to get my hole to accept his thumb knuckle. "I love a challenge. Now *stop* moving." He dug his fingers into my neck to get me to stay still.

I yelped as he started pushing harder, gradually forcing me open, and I started sobbing in fright. I was having flashbacks to the first time he raped me. It was the same excruciating pain, the same fear that I was torn and bleeding. "No no no no no." My voice was hoarse between my gasps. "No no n—" I screamed as his knuckle passed the threshold, his hand pulled right into me up to the wrist by the constricting ring of muscle. Goosebumps broke out over my entire body as I thrashed in agony, impaled on his fist, my hole pulsing and burning.

"See? No sweat," Mitch said, but when he moved his hand inside me, I screamed again.

"Don't. Don't. Don't," I begged, gulping for air as my head swam.

"What? You want me to take it out?" Mitch gave a low, teasing laugh. "Why didn't you say so?"

My body went rigid as he started pulling his hand out of me, the pain mounting again as the skin began stretching, and this time, it was too much for me.

My brain shut down, and I was gone.

When I woke up, I found he'd successfully taken his fist out of my ass and had gone back to fucking me. I had no idea how long I'd been unconscious, but from the way he was panting, he'd been at it a while now. My ass was numb. My mind was numb. Nothing mattered. I didn't let on that I was awake; I just waited for him to finish and leave. Then, when he was finally gone, I turned on my side and tried to cry, but the tears wouldn't come.

I decided to jerk off instead.

It was only after I'd cum that my tears finally broke through, the release almost as intense as an orgasm. As I lay there sobbing, my phone buzzed twice. Wiping my face, I read the messages from Mitch:

> Hey sleeping beauty I'll be back for more after my shift 👮🥒

> Have supper ready

> Make pasta

I shook my head and, jaw clenched, typed a message back:

Fine.

He replied immediately:

Good boy

I just stared, hating myself for how warm my cheeks were in response to his words.

I didn't reply.

CHAPTER 4
DETOUR

SEPTEMBER

"WHERE *YOU* OFF TO?"

I jumped at the sound of Mitch's voice and looked behind me, bumping into a no-parking sign and nearly falling off the sidewalk in the process. Mitch was leaning out the window of his police cruiser with a grin.

"I have to go to the pharmacy," I mumbled, clutching the strap of my bag with both hands as I turned and hurried away.

"Hop in! I'll give you a lift," Mitch said cheerfully, his squad car keeping pace with me.

"No, thank you."

"It's no problem." *Please, please leave me the fuck alone.*

"Get in . . . the fucking . . . car, Patrick"

There was no point in arguing. Shoulders slumped, I gritted my teeth and sighed, then did as I was told. He always made me sit in the back. I think he liked the fact that I was trapped back there.

Whistling along with the radio, Mitch drove me the ten blocks to the pharmacy, then let me out of the backseat with a little chivalrous gesture and a mocking smile.

"Hey, why don't you grab some lube while you're in there, champ? You're running low," he said, leaning against the side of the car, crossing his arms over his chest. He scratched the side of his jaw, his stubble making an audible rasp as he tilted his head at me, eyes narrowed. "And then I'll give you a lift back. Sound good?"

Nodding numbly, I went inside. I felt like crying. He wouldn't *just* drop me off at home and leave. *Fuck.* My ass still hurt from that morning's visit, but I was *always* sore. He was inside me so often it felt like a compulsion. And it was never done gently or with any care for me at all.

Maybe he'll get bored and leave if I dawdle long enough here? I clenched my jaw as I stared at the shelves of shampoo. More likely, he'd come and get me. *And* he'd be pissed off. It would hurt even more then.

I quickly found the bottle I was looking for, then jogged to the cash, cursed to myself, and doubled back to grab some lube. Mitch *was* right—I was almost out, and if I didn't have enough on hand, he'd just use spit instead. My ass couldn't take that.

I usually bought cheap pharmacy-brand lube but decided to buy the best one they had in stock instead. As I stood at the cash, I imagined an ad with a voiceover: "Use Astroglide . . . for a smoother, more *pleasurable* rape."

I snorted and the guy ringing me up gave me a funny look.

"Uhh . . . where are we going?" I asked nervously as Mitch drove in the opposite direction from my apartment.

"A call came in while you were taking your sweet time dicking around in there. I just need to go check on something."

"Oh. Okay." I chewed on the corner of my lip, watching the buildings fly by as we headed west.

"Ah. There she is."

An elderly woman was sitting on a bench in front of an office building wearing nothing but a floral housecoat and slippers. Mitch pulled over and stopped in front of her.

"Mrs. Sinclair?" he said, smiling as he got out of the cruiser.

The woman looked up, her expression vague and unfocused. She blinked at the cop a few times, then broke into a delighted smile. "Gary?"

"No, ma'am. I'm Officer McKenzie, but you can call me Mitch if you like." He held his hand out to the woman. "Your daughter is *very* worried about you."

"You look *just* like my son Gary," Mrs. Sinclair replied, taking his hand. "Do you know him?"

"No, ma'am. But why don't you tell me about him while we take a little drive."

"Drive?" Her face went blank with confusion again, and then she furrowed her brow, waving a frail hand towards the bench. "No, no. I'm waiting for my husband. The train will be here soon, and I wanted to surprise him."

Mitch smiled and gently put his arm around the elderly woman's back, steering her towards the cop car.

"Are you cold? Nights are getting chillier now, eh? I can turn on the heat if you like," he said, seating her in the passenger side. Without waiting for her reply, he clicked on the heat and fastened her safety belt. "There. All settled now. We'll get you home in a jiffy."

"Oh?" she replied, staring out the window. "Oh." She mumbled something else and then nodded. "Yes, I think that's for the best." She was silent for a few minutes as Mitch drove, then turned to look at him. "Oh! You know, you look just like my son Gary," she said, repeating herself. "Do you know him?"

"No, ma'am, but sounds like he's a handsome fella."

Mrs. Sinclair laughed. "He is! So handsome . . . *Just* like his father. And such a good boy. You know he— Oh!" She noticed me in the back seat and craned her neck to get a better look at me. "Who is that boy? Is he a criminal?"

"Yes, ma'am," Mitch replied, shooting me a smirk in the rearview. "He was caught with his pants down in public."

"Oh my." Mrs. Sinclair's mouth hung open as she stared at me, and I averted my gaze, my face burning.

Mitch chuckled, meeting my eyes again in the mirror. "Yep. He's a naughty boy, all right."

We drove Mrs. Sinclair back home where her daughter was waiting tearfully on the front steps. Mitch helped the elderly woman out of the car, then stood chatting with the pair for a good fifteen minutes. Meanwhile, I was getting uncomfortably warm because he'd left the heat on and I couldn't roll down the windows.

Asshole.

Finally, the conversation wrapped up, and Mitch wrote something in his pad, handing the paper to the daughter. She nodded and smiled. Then Mitch *hugged* her.

Huh.

"Yeah, you too," Mitch said cheerfully as he opened the car door. "Stay safe!" He slid behind the wheel and buckled in. "Hoo boy. A little sweaty back there?" he asked as he turned off the heat. "Sorry about that, buddy." He cracked the windows in the back.

It was weird . . . like Mitch's personality had done a sudden one-eighty. We drove in silence for a little while, and then I cleared my throat.

"That was nice of you. With the old lady."

Mitch's eyes met mine in the rearview. "Yeah, well, helping out old bats like that is part of the job."

Aaaannd we're back to the old Mitch. I frowned.

"What? Did you think I did it out of the kindness of my heart?" He laughed, focusing on the road again.

"Is it your job to give out hugs too?" I asked dryly.

"Hey, did you *see* the tits on that blonde? How could I *not* give her a squeeze?" He grinned. "I gave her my number in case she needed anything. I hope to *Christ* she calls. I'd love to see those tits jiggle while she's bouncing in my lap." His gaze met mine again, and a little wrinkle formed between his dark brows as he scrutinized me for an uncomfortably long moment.

Uh oh. "What?"

Mitch didn't reply. A few streets later, he slowed, then threw the car in reverse and turned.

"What are you doing?" It looked like he was backing into a blind alleyway between an art gallery and a high-end home decor shop, both closed for the night. My heart leapt in my chest, and I let out a ragged breath. *Shit.* "Uh, Mitch?"

Mitch killed the engine and engaged the parking brake, then got out and opened my door. "Out." He had to hold onto the car door so that it wouldn't hit the brick wall, and it effectively blocked any chance I had of making a run for it.

I nervously got out.

"Go on." He growled, pointing to the back of the pitch-dark alleyway.

"Why?"

"Just do it."

There was about four or five feet of clearance between the wall and the cruiser's back bumper, and I could just barely see a door set into the brick. Confused, I wondered if that was where he wanted me to go, but as I felt around, searching for a knob, Mitch grabbed me by the shoulder and turned me around.

"Where the fuck do you think you're going?" he asked, pushing me back towards the police cruiser. He shoved me against the trunk, bending me over so that my head smacked the rear window, then yanked down my shorts and boxers with one hand while holding me down with the other.

I heard the snap of a lid, and I whimpered. "Mitch. Please."

"Mitch, please," he repeated in a mocking tone, laughing. "How about I stick my Maglite up your ass to get things started? Would you like that?"

"N-no. Please."

"Here." I heard him fumble with something. "Say ahh."

Confused, I did as I was told, and when he placed something between my teeth, it took me a second to realize it was the little leatherbound notepad he kept in his breast pocket.

"Bite on that. I don't want you making a fucking noise."

Oh god. I bit down on the pad as his lubed-up cock touched my swollen, tender hole—I had tears in my eyes even before he started forcing his dick into me. I let out a high-pitched whine as his cockhead spread me open, and he stopped, grabbing my arm to wrench it behind me. He held onto my thumb, squeezing the base of it.

"Feel this?" he asked. "If you make another *fucking* sound, this is where your thumb will dislocate. Understood?" He gave another hard squeeze, and I nodded, then added a mangled *yes* around the notebook in my mouth, just in case he couldn't see my nod in the dark.

Mitch added more lube, wetting his shaft up to where it was buried in my throbbing hole, then gave a hard push, sliding himself further in. I exhaled, trembling with the effort of holding back my cries, and crushed my eyes closed, praying for it to be over quickly.

With the help of more lube and effort, Mitch managed to get most of his cock into me, then started fucking me hard and fast, shaking the car so much that it began to creak in time to his thrusts.

"Fuck." Mitch suddenly stopped moving, and I thought maybe he had cum, but when I lifted my head, I saw a group of people walking by the mouth of the alleyway. I could cry out for help.

I should. . . right? But I didn't.

Once the group had passed, Mitch resumed fucking me, but this time slower and with less force, presumably to keep the squad car from making too much noise.

Oh god. I realized it was starting, that thing that made no sense. The shameful, awful thing that kept happening.

I was getting hard.

Here I was, my ass painfully stretched to its limit and my shoulder *screaming* from having my arm twisted behind me, and for some unfathomable reason, my now rock-hard boner was happily sliding against the back of the car, evidently lubed up by the precum that was leaking out of it.

And, worse . . . I was already close.

I panted quickly through my nose with the notepad clenched in my teeth and grimaced as Mitch started leaning into his thrusts again. It didn't take long before he hilted himself and stopped, letting out a staccato sigh as his dick jerked and twitched inside me. I pushed back into him as he loaded my ass, barely holding back a cry as I started to cum, my raw hole pulsing around the thick shaft buried inside me. I'd barely finished when he released me and pulled out, and my knees buckled, so I grabbed onto the trunk of the car. Legs quaking, I rested my cheek on the cool glass and tried to get my breathing under control.

"The fuck was *that?*" Mitch asked, sounding amused. "Did you just do what I think you did?"

I pulled the notepad out of my mouth and winced. My jaw was sore. I slowly pushed myself off the car's trunk as Mitch clicked on his flashlight.

He pointed the beam at my groin and laughed. "Holy shit."

Shamefaced, I pulled my boxers and shorts back up as he watched. The material stuck uncomfortably to my cum-covered thighs.

Then he turned his flashlight on the car and shook his head. "Oh man. And it was *just* detailed this morning." He clicked his tongue disapprovingly.

An impressive amount of cum dripped from the rear panel, down over the license plate, and onto the navy-blue bumper.

"Well. Go on. Clean it up."

"Uh, with what?" I asked, shifting uncomfortably in my wet boxers.

"Use your tongue." He let out a growly little chuckle.

"*What?*" I looked over at Mitch, but his face was obscured because of the bright light in my eyes. I couldn't tell if he was being serious. "I'm not doing that."

"Yes, you fucking *are*," he said and grabbed me by the shoulder, forcing me down on my knees. "Lick it up, you little shit." Then he grabbed a handful of my hair and shoved my face into the mess.

With tears in my eyes, I started lapping up my cold cum, coughing and gagging every time I swallowed. It felt like forever before he was satisfied. Finally, I was allowed to get to my feet, and I used my T-shirt to wipe the tears and cum and dirt off my face. My tongue felt gritty, so I wiped it too.

Mitch startled me by suddenly cupping my groin, snickering when he found that my dick was half hard again.

"Thought so," he said, shining the light in my face, blinding me. "You little freak."

I shielded my eyes, my face hot with shame as he fondled me until I had a full-blown erection.

"Damn. You look like a bitch in heat." Mitch laughed again and released me after giving my dick one last squeeze. Then he frowned, reaching for something on the squad car's trunk. It was his notepad. He shone the beam on it and grinned at the clear indentations my teeth had left.

"A little memento of our time together, eh?" he said and slid the pad into his breast pocket, giving it a little pat. After clicking off the flashlight, Mitch went to the driver's side door and opened it. He looked back at me. "Get in."

I didn't move. "Where are we going?"

Mitch stared at me like I was a complete moron. "I'm driving you home, dumbass."

"You are?"

"What? Did you think I was just going to abandon you here? It's not a safe part of town."

I raised my eyebrows. Not a safe part of town? From where I

stood, I could see two Teslas and a Beemer parked across from the alleyway.

"Jesus H. Christ, Patrick. Just get in the *fucking* car, will you?" He waited until I was in the backseat before getting in himself, muttering quietly as he shook his head, then he watched me by the slowly dimming light of the dome while I did up my seatbelt.

As Mitch pulled out of the alleyway, he said, "I ought to spank that scrawny ass of yours." Then he scoffed. "Though you'd like that, wouldn't you?" His eyes smiled at me in the rearview. "Yeah, you probably *loved* it when your mommy gave you a good spanking. *Oh*, wait . . . *no*." He laughed softly. "That's right . . . you'd only get a boner when *Daddy* was spanking you, wouldn't you? That's probably why you turned out gay, huh?"

I knew he was taunting me just to get a rise out of me. I couldn't believe that Mitch was dumb enough to think you could be "turned" gay. I shook my head and sighed, staring out the side window.

"I was never spanked as a kid," I said quietly.

"What? *Never?*"

I glanced at the rearview where he held my gaze, his brows high.

"Nope," I replied.

Mitch snorted and turned his focus back to his driving. "Well, no wonder you're so goddamn soft." He sucked his teeth, and I noticed his hands tighten on the steering wheel. "*Christ*. My dad used to beat the living tar out of me all the fucking time." He said it like he was proud.

"That's awful," I replied, trying to keep the sarcasm out of my voice.

"Awful? *Nah*." He hit the brakes hard at the next intersection and waited maybe three seconds before groaning impatiently. He then reached down and touched a switch, causing the siren to squawk twice before he ran the red light. "One time, when I was maybe six or seven, my dad caught me dancing to one of Mum's

Bowie albums. Broke my arm right here"—he touched his left forearm about halfway up—"because he didn't want me turning out the way you did."

"Good for you." I met his eyes in the mirror again, keeping my expression neutral.

Mitch frowned and drove the rest of the way in silence.

CHAPTER 5
FUCKBOY

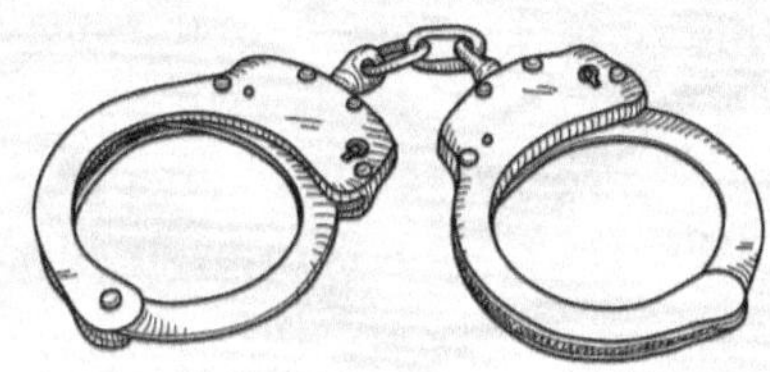

OCTOBER

"I've never fucked a guy before, though."

"A hole is a hole, Dave. And my fuckboy's hole feels just like a pussy. You'll see," replied Mitch, slapping my ass.

Dave looked at me dubiously, stroking his beard.

I turned away, humiliated and miserable. I was naked, on my hands and knees on the motel bed, my hole being inspected by the trio of friends Mitch had brought with him.

"He doesn't look too happy," Dave pointed out.

"He *always* looks like that."

"I dunno." Dave sighed audibly. "I don't think I can do this, man."

"Hey, it's your loss. I just thought you'd wanna get laid for once. Just stay and watch for a bit. I'm sure it'll get your dick hard."

"All right. Fine."

"Hell *yeah*, Dave. Let's *do* this." This came from Rob, a tall, skinny guy with a buzz cut and a cop moustache. He pulled a baggie out of his vest and held it up. "Anyone want a bump?"

"Fuck *yes*," replied Mitch, laughing.

The last guy, whom Mitch had called Ti-Louis, only nodded. Grey-haired and sallow-skinned, he was gaunt and scarred and had this *look* in his eyes as he watched me silently. He was creepy as hell.

Rob was the first to put his dick in me. Then it was Ti-Louis. The two of them took turns with me between snorting lines of coke until Dave finally joined in. Since none of the guys were as girthy as Mitch, my mouth also got a lot of use. Half an hour into the "fun," a fourth guy named Pierre showed up with a litre of Jameson. He sniffed a line of coke right off my back as he fucked me. None of them wore a condom.

Through all of this, Mitch didn't join in. He'd done a little coke at the beginning and joked around with the guys, but then had stretched out on the other bed just to watch. I kept glancing over at him because something was just . . . *off*. He saw me looking and took a pull from the bottle of whiskey, then turned away. Was he bored? Or was it something else? Was he *angry?*

Worried that I'd get punished later for not putting on a better show, I gave a little moan, pretending to enjoy what was being done to me, even though my dick was softer than a wet noodle.

"Mitch, can we double-fuck him?"

"Sure. Why not." He sounded completely disinterested. A moment later, he actually turned on the television.

Meanwhile, Pierre and Rob were trying to decide what was the least "gay" way to both put their dicks in me.

"Nah, man, I don't want your fucking balls touching mine," Rob said when Pierre suggested that I stay on my hands and knees with one of them below and the other above.

"Or you could do like . . . here . . ." Dave said, joining in on the discussion. "Pierre, you fuck him like this, okay?"

Pierre slid his cock into my hole, and I closed my eyes with a sigh.

"Okay, now Rob can straddle him from the top and put his dick in over yours."

Rob stepped up on the bed and threw a leg over me, but Pierre stepped back, pulling out. "No way. I don't want to stare at your fucking hairy asshole."

Finally, they had me lie on my side between them so they could put their cocks in me without their balls touching. Or touching *much*. I felt like pointing out that they were going to literally rub their cocks together inside me, but I kept my mouth shut.

Rob put his dick in me first, helpfully holding my leg up, then Pierre joined him from behind me. The combined girth of their two dicks was less than Mitch's thick cock, but it was still a stretch, and I let out a pained grunt.

"Shit, is this hurting you?" Rob asked. His dark brown, bloodshot eyes were wide with honest concern.

Looking for guidance, my eyes flicked to Mitch, and I found him staring at me with his jaw set and his brows low. *Shit.*

"Uh. No. No, it's fine," I said quickly, wincing as Pierre's dick opened me up more. "It feels good. *Really* . . . huhhh . . . good."

Pierre didn't last very long. He ended up cumming all over Rob's dick, which Rob didn't seem to mind. Then Dave took Pierre's place.

I might have enjoyed having two cum-covered cocks pistoning in my hole if I hadn't been forced into it by my tormentor, but as it was, I felt like an object. A piece of trash. But then again, I felt the same when Mitch fucked me . . . didn't I?

I closed my eyes again and waited for them to finish.

Ti-Louis had already cum earlier in the evening, so I was surprised when he stepped up for another turn once Dave and Rob were done crossing swords.

He flipped me onto my back and jammed his cock into my hole, fucking me as deep as his little dick could get while staring at me with this crazed look in his eyes. I was so distracted that I didn't even notice the others had gone until the motel door slammed shut—when I looked over, I saw that it was just the three of us left. Mitch barely spared me a glance before changing the channel to some show where a woman lay bleeding in a bathtub.

I was startled when Ti-Louis suddenly paused to wrap his hands around my throat. He squeezed, and I rasped in a breath, my eyes darting to Mitch, wondering what I was supposed to do, but all his focus was on the TV.

As Ti-Louis resumed fucking me with renewed vigour, I grasped at the duvet to either side of me, struggling to breathe and hoping he'd be done with me soon. But then he began leaning into his grasp, tightening his hold on me until black shapes crept into my vision. I was going to suffocate. I grabbed his wrists, trying to fight him off, and managed to let out a rattling wheeze.

"Hey! That's enough," Mitch said, finally noticing what was happening. "*C'est assez!*"

I stared helplessly, my eyes bulging as I clawed at Ti-Louis's wrists, but by the time Mitch stood to come to my rescue, presumably, Ti-Louis released me and stared off to the side, his yellowed teeth clenched, quietly seeding my hole for the second time that night.

Ti-Louis pulled out and yanked his pants back up, then snagged the last of the coke from the bedside table and left the motel room without a word or backward glance.

I lay there gasping, unnerved by what had happened, but when I looked over, Mitch had gone back to the other bed, ignoring me while he watched TV and drank whiskey.

I frowned and sat up, watching him for a few moments. "What's wrong?"

"Nothing."

"Did I do something?"

Mitch turned to me, his expression frustratingly blank. "No," he said, then went back to his show.

"So . . . uh . . . those are your friends, eh?" I said awkwardly.

"They're not my friends."

"Oh." Chewing the corner of my lip, I stayed quiet until there was a commercial break. Then I cleared my throat.

"Um. Were you going to fuck me?"

Lip curled, Mitch looked over at me. "With your pussy full of their spunk? No fucking thank you."

I stared at him wide-eyed. Had I completely misunderstood the goal of the little gangbang he'd planned? I was so confused.

"I mean, it's, uh, totally fine if you, like, don't want to . . ." I stammered. *How the fuck did I get to this point?* It was insanity. "I just thought . . . You know . . ."

After staring at me for a few seconds, Mitch heaved a sigh. "Here." He picked up a half-empty bottle of water from the floor and tossed it at me. "Go rinse yourself out."

"Oh. Okay." I nodded. "I'll be quick."

"Hm." Mitch turned his focus back on the television.

In the bathroom, I gave myself a thorough but shallow rinse, refilling the water bottle several times until no more cum came out of me, and my hole no longer felt slick when I slid two fingers into it to check. Hoping it was enough to satisfy Mitch, I washed my hands and face, then stared at myself in the mirror.

You look like shit. My blue eyes looked wild in their dark, sunken sockets, and my dirty-blond hair looked almost brown because of how pasty white my skin was.

Well, I'm not pasty everywhere. I touched the red welts around my neck. They'd turn into bruises, I was certain. *Fuck.* I guess I was lucky to be alive.

I noticed then that Mitch's toiletries were laid out neatly by the sink and lifted an eyebrow. *Weird. How long is he planning on staying here?* I'd assumed he'd only rented the room to pimp me out to his pals, and then he'd go home afterwards . . . but then why would he bring all this stuff? Lined up next to a black leather toiletry kit was a stick of sporty-scented deodorant, a toothbrush and toothpaste, a comb, a small tin of hair pomade, tweezers, nail clippers, some fancy unscented face cream, a shaving brush, and a razor with a polished wooden handle. I picked up the expensive-looking razor and frowned at it. Then I noticed the hand soap—there was only a tiny sliver left.

Perplexed, I put the razor carefully back in its place and saw something in the mirror's reflection. I turned around and found a pair of socks and black boxer briefs hanging in the shower, drying, and the trash can next to the toilet was full. *Huh.*

I left the bathroom quietly and took a peek in the closet. Hanging inside were Mitch's uniform and a couple of spare work shirts, a few pairs of pants neatly draped over hangers, and about a dozen long and short-sleeved button-downs. Black boots like the ones Mitch wore to work were in the bottom of the closet, along with some tattered dark-blue sneakers . . . and a pair of sunshine-yellow flip-flops. I grinned—I could *not* imagine Mitch wearing flip-flops, much less in yellow.

Turning to the dresser under the TV, I frowned. If I opened the drawers, I *knew* I'd find the rest of Mitch's clothes. I cleared my throat.

"Mitch?"

"What?"

"Um. Are you, uh, living here?" I asked quietly.

Mitch stared at me for so long without moving that it felt eerily like time had stopped. A muscle in his cheek twitched. *Uh oh.* My heart started stuttering in my ribcage. *Shit.*

He lifted the bottle of whiskey to his lips and took a long pull before narrowing his eyes at me.

"That's none of your *fucking* business," he said in a low, restrained voice.

"You're right . . . you're totally right," I said, my mouth suddenly dry. I gave a fearful little chuckle. "I shouldn't have said anything. I mean, I don't even know why I asked that." I held up my hands as his eyes continued to bore into me. "I mean, I was *curious,* but that doesn't mean I should have *said* anything. At all. About anything." I couldn't stop babbling as the muscles visibly bulged in his jaw as he clenched his teeth. "Really. I'm so—"

"Get on the fucking bed." His voice was deathly quiet, but it might as well have been a shout.

I dove towards the other bed and sat down, watching as he rose unsteadily to his feet, still clutching the bottle as he approached.

"The fuck are you doing? Get on your fucking knees, dipshit."

I rolled over and popped up on my knees, my heart hammering my ribcage. I heard the whiskey slosh in the bottle and Mitch swallowing audibly. Then I gasped and flinched as his cold hand touched my ass.

Closing my eyes, I braced myself, but when he hadn't put his dick in me after a few very long minutes had passed, I grew confused. I heard Mitch mutter to himself and glanced over my shoulder to see what was happening. He was looking down, and from the sounds of it, he was jerking himself off. From his frustrated expression, I guessed he was having trouble getting hard.

Mitch noticed me watching and made a harsh noise in the back of his throat.

"Don't fucking look at me."

I quickly averted my gaze and waited, listening to him grumble under his breath as he worked on his cock. Finally, he got himself hard enough to penetrate me, but only barely because as soon as he began thrusting, his half-limp dick slipped right out.

"*Fuck.*" He grabbed hold of my hips, roughly jerking me backwards before the sounds of him stroking himself resumed. "Your cunt's so fucking loose I can't feel a fucking thing."

I frowned. "Um . . ." I chewed my lip as Mitch attempted to stuff his cock into me again, to no avail.

"Stop fucking moving!" After a few more tries, he let out an exasperated growl. "Know what? Forget it. Fuckin' forget it. Didn't wanna fuck your dirty faggot whore ass anyway," he said, slurring his words as he walked away. "C'mon, dipshit. Gonna drive you home."

Alarmed, I straightened up to look at him. "Uh, I don't think that's a good idea, Mitch. You've had a *lot* to drink." Even as I was saying them, I *knew* my words were a mistake.

Mitch's eyes widened. "*What* did you fuckin' say?" He lunged at me, grabbing a handful of my hair. "You think I can't fucking handle my liquor?"

Whimpering, I clutched at his wrist as he pulled me off the bed, terrified he'd rip my hair out along with part of my scalp, and tried to get my knees under me as he dragged me across the dirty carpet. Mitch then yanked open the door, hauled me painfully to my feet, and pushed me out of the motel room into the parking lot. I flew out onto the cold pavement as the door slammed behind me, skinning both my knees and hands as I landed badly. Gasping in pain, I quickly scrabbled to my feet and ran back to the door, pressing my nakedness against it with one hand covering my bare backside.

"Mitch?" I whispered into the seam between the door and doorframe, softly rapping on the peeling paint with my fingertips. I didn't dare knock louder—I didn't want to call attention to myself. The motel was right off a major street, with a 24-hour depanneur next to it and a still-open diner right across the street. As I stood there shivering and naked for all the world to see, a car turned into the dep's parking lot. *Fuck.* There was nowhere to hide. Worse, I was clearly visible to anyone passing by because of the moth-swarmed light above me.

"Mitch?" I tried again, tapping quietly. "It was a joke. I didn't mean it. *Mitch?* Mitch, please? I'm sorry. I didn't mean to imply you were drunk." I glanced over my shoulder as another car approached, slowing. "I'm really, *really* sorry."

It wouldn't be long before someone called the cops.

Call the cops? It's a cop that put you out on your bare ass, idiot. I clawed back the hysterical giggles that threatened to burst free.

"Mitch?" I rasped hoarsely, pressing my lips to the door crack. I squeezed my eyes shut, praying I could get through to him. "*Please* let me in?"

I stumbled forward, almost falling on my face when Mitch suddenly pulled open the door.

"Thank you," I said breathlessly, shutting the door behind me and leaning back against it. I panted in relief. "Oh my god. Thank you, thank you, thank you."

Mitch didn't even look at me. He just grunted and re-installed himself in front of the television.

I stood there in awkward silence as he continued to ignore me, wondering what to say. Finally, I held up my gritty, scuffed palms. "I'm . . . um, I'm just going to use the sink to clean up. Is that okay?"

When he didn't reply, I picked up my clothes and shuffled quickly past him, apologizing for obstructing his view, and ducked into the bathroom. I closed the door and let out a slow, ragged breath.

Volatile fucking asshole. Jesus. I wish I knew what I had done to piss him off so much. I could understand him being embarrassed about living at a motel, and I knew better than to criticize him about anything—I *really* should have kept my mouth shut—but it wasn't just that. He'd been acting so weird all night. Mitch was over-the-top aggressive, yes. But there was always some humour in it. *Usually* at my expense. This? This was different. I'd seen him get annoyed or impatient a shitload of times, but it wasn't until just then that I realized I'd never seen him get truly *angry* before. And that's what he was . . . angry.

I couldn't wait to get the hell out of there.

Using Mitch's tweezers, I quickly removed as much gravel from my hands and knees as I could. Then, I used some antibiotic ointment that I found in Mitch's toiletry kit before getting dressed. I pocketed the tube, figuring Mitch owed me, and used his comb to make myself look halfway decent.

"I'm going to catch the bus," I said as I left the bathroom, but I realized I was talking to myself. Mitch was passed out on the bed, snoring, with the nearly empty bottle of whiskey still clutched in his hand. I stared down at him for a moment, then grabbed the whiskey and took a big swig of it, swishing it around in my mouth before spitting it back into the bottle. "Have some backwash, fucker," I whispered, leaving the whiskey on the bedside table. I eyed Mitch's keys and thought about borrowing his crappy old turd-brown Corolla to get home but figured he would beat the shit out of me if I did.

Grabbing my jacket, I turned to leave, but when I reached for the doorknob, I just stood there with my eyes closed.

Just go.

Just. Go.

I sighed. Jaw clenched, I backtracked and flipped the hanging edge of the duvet up to cover Mitch and gently nudged his head into a better position so he wouldn't wake up with a sore neck. Then I left.

In the end, I decided not to take the bus. It took me over twenty minutes by foot, but the crisp fall air helped to clear my head. By the time I got home, I figured I was overthinking things like usual, and Mitch had probably just had a bad day or something and wasn't really angry at *me*. Because . . . what did I do wrong?

Yeah, he'll probably be in a better mood when I see him after work tomorrow, I thought as I climbed into bed. At least, I hoped he would be.

CHAPTER 6
GHOSTED

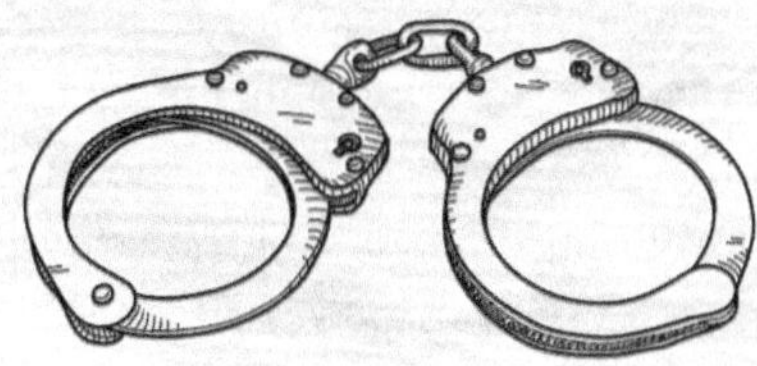

MITCH DIDN'T COME over after work the next day. Nor the day after. I stood at my cash register, chewing the corner of my lip as I stared at the text message I had composed:

> Is everything all right?

I frowned, erased it, and typed out a new one:

> Hello?

Rubbing the back of my neck, I locked my phone and dropped it into my apron, message unsent. *Why* the *fuck* would I reach out to him?

A customer appeared, and I rang the woman up, but I was so distracted that I accidentally charged her twice for her Halloween candy. I apologized and refunded the woman, then went back to staring at my phone when she had gone.

I backspaced and wrote:

> Still alive? ;)

"You okay?" Maude folded her arms over the top of the divider and rested her chin on them. "You seem glum, chum."

Fuck it. I hit Send and quickly pocketed my phone. "I'm fine," I replied a little defensively. *Jesus. What's the matter with me? I should be* happy *that I'm getting a nice break from being his bitch.*

"You sure?" Maude tilted her head, her dark brown eyes crinkling at the corners as she smiled at me. "How are things with the boyfriend?"

I shrugged. "Everything fine," I said, resisting the urge to check to see if Mitch had seen my message yet. "I think."

"Uh oh. Trouble in paradise?"

I snorted. "Um, 'paradise' is definitely *not* how I would describe my relationship with Mitch . . . if you can even call it that."

"Oh?"

Normally, I fended off her questions about Mitch with vague non-answers, but not hearing from him for two days was doing something weird to my brain. For once, I actually *wanted* to open up to someone about what I'd been going through.

"It's more like an . . . arrangement."

"Oh yeah? So, he's like, your sugar daddy?" Her grin widened.

Grimacing, I shook my head. "No. More like . . . my ass belongs to him, and there's nothing I can do about it?"

Maude's eyes went round as she stood up straight. "Uh, that's a big yikes."

"Yeah. I know."

"So, he just uses you for sex?"

"Pretty much."

"I mean, the man is *sexy*, but that is sus as fuck. What do *you* get out of it?"

I stared at her for a moment in silence. I had no idea what to say. I obviously was getting something out of it, or else I wouldn't be stressing out about his unexplained absence.

"It's . . . complicated?" I finally answered. *Argh.*

"Seriously, Pat, if he's treating you like shit, dump his ass."

"Dump whose ass? The cop?" Khadim looked up from refilling the paper bags at the express cash.

"Yeah. He's just using Pat for sex," Maude replied.

My cheeks grew warm as I avoided Khadim's eyes.

"Well, that makes it even grosser," he said, then sucked his teeth and shook his head as he went back to his task.

"Wait, why gross-*er*?" I asked, frowning. "Why do you think it's gross?"

Khadim's shoulder came up in a tiny shrug, and his forehead creased as he met my gaze.

"I mean, the dude is like twice your age, isn't he?" His lip curled. "I kinda find that pervy, don't you?"

I blinked. "Uh . . ."

"*Hey*, there's nothing wrong with being into older guys," Maude said. "I've dated plenty of older guys, and I wouldn't call it pervy."

"Okay. How old was the oldest guy you dated?" Khadim stood, crossing his arms as he cocked his head at Maude.

"Thirty-two."

Khadim smirked and turned to me. "And how old is the cop?"

"I . . . I actually don't know," I stammered. "It's never come up." I squinted, thinking. "I know he graduated high school in '91."

"Okay, so he was out of high school before you were even *born*?" Khadim made a face. "Unless the dude is some kind of genius and graduated early, that means he's like . . . fifty. *More* than twice your age."

"He doesn't *look* fifty," Maude interjected, pulling her long ponytail over her shoulder to stroke it hand over hand as her gaze went distant. She was obviously picturing Mitch in her head. "Maybe, like, mid-forties."

"Still. He's an old guy using a kid for sex." Khadim arched an eyebrow at me. "See? Perv."

"I'm not a kid," I replied.

"I'm older than you and still consider myself a kid."

I scowled at Khadim. "Well, I don't. And I'm not. And it's not *like* that."

"So what's it like, then? You said he was using you for sex, right?" He glanced at Maude and she nodded.

"Yeah. But . . ." I stared at both of them for a moment with my jaw clenched tight, regretting having brought up Mitch to begin with. I cleared my throat. "But, it's more *complicated* than that. And age doesn't matter to me. That's not an issue." Why the hell was I defending my relationship with Mitch? *I need to get my head checked.* "It's not like that," I repeated. "It's . . . uh . . . different."

"Oh *wait*, is this like . . . a BDSM thing?" Maude asked, perking up. "Is that what you're trying to say."

I just stood there gnawing on my lower lip for a moment, then sighed and shrugged, giving up.

"Yeah. It's that kind of thing." I gave Maude a tight smile. "I just find it, uh, weird to talk about, you know?"

"Gotcha."

"Nope. Don't care. Still pervy," Khadim said, reaching up to slap the Cash/*Caisse* sign hanging above him as he walked away. The sign creaked as it swayed, and Maude rolled her eyes as she went back to leaning on the divider between our stations.

"Khad probably thinks anything other than missionary is pervy," she said, grinning. "Soooo, well, *that's* hot and kinky. Go you!" She reached out and booped my nose with her finger. "Didn't know you had it in you."

I chuckled awkwardly, desperately wanting to shut down the conversation.

"So, how does it work? Like, he wants you to be his own personal sex slave?" She bit her bottom lip and widened her eyes.

"Basically," I said, my face burning.

"And it's all consensual?"

"Yep." As I said it, something unsettling dawned on me: *it wasn't totally a lie.* My eyes lost focus, and I stood there, barely breathing. Could I no longer tell the difference between *tolerating* the shit Mitch did to me and *consenting* to it?

I blinked, horrified to realize that somewhere along the way, I'd apparently stopped considering it outright rape.

Heart pounding, I quickly dug into my apron pocket and pulled out my phone. "Oh shit. It's him," I said, pretending a call was coming in. "I should really get this. Be right back." I pressed the phone to my ear as I fled, heading towards the back of the store. In the empty breakroom, I sat on one of the cheap foldout chairs and stared down at my phone, nervously thumbing open the messaging app.

Mitch had seen my message but hadn't replied. I frowned and force-quit the app in case it was glitching, but when the message screen came back up, my text was still marked read with no reply. Two days without a visit, and now he was ignoring my texts?

Maybe he's just busy. I chewed the inside of my cheek, scrolling through dozens of messages between us. Mitch *always* answered.

What the fuck?

I frowned, thumb hovering over the keyboard.

No. Don't do it. Grow a fucking spine. Why do you care *if he's not answering you? Maybe he's still pissed at you. Maybe he's just sick of you. Who fucking cares? Either way, you're free. You should be* happy *he's ignoring you, you stupid piece of shit.* I groaned softly, then tapped out another message:

> Are you mad at me?

I hit Send and then shook my head. *Pathetic.*

A week went by without a word from Mitch. My messages went unanswered. When I tried calling the police station a few times, they said he was either busy or out.

I lost my appetite. I called in sick at work.

Every cruiser that passed by my window filled me with such hope and dread that I felt like throwing up, and then I cried when they didn't stop.

In a word, I was miserable.

And I *hated* myself for it. There wasn't a single person on the planet who loathed themselves more than I loathed myself for how I was reacting to being ghosted by Mitch.

Mitch the rapist. Mitch the bully. Mitch the fucking assho— I fumbled my phone when it suddenly buzzed in my hand, then sighed in disgust at how disappointed I was that it was just some Uber Eats promotion. I turned over on my back and stared at the ceiling.

"Nuh-uh. Don't," I muttered as an idea took root. A really fucking *stupid* idea. "Don't even *think* about it." I shook my head, squeezing my eyes shut. "Just . . . *don't.*"

CHAPTER 7
BUT I DID IT ANYWAY

NOVEMBER

I STOOD between the glass doors for a few moments, my heart beating so hard I felt faint.

"This is a bad idea, Patrick," I whispered. "This is *such* a bad idea." I knew I should turn around and go home. Maybe pick up some beer or weed on the way and get good and wasted. And after that, I would look up the name of a good psychologist. That would be the *smart* thing to do.

Instead, I took a deep breath and pulled open the inside door, stepping into the quiet police station. I swallowed, staring at the uniformed woman behind the tall, putty-coloured front desk. She had her head down, probably looking at her phone. I glanced left, where there was a long hallway with blue doors, then quickly looked right when I heard voices. Someone gave a hoarse laugh beyond the big grey double doors, and the sounds grew quieter as another door closed in the distance.

"*Puis-je vous aider?* Can I help you?"

Startled, I turned to the woman and stared at her long enough that her welcoming smile faded and a wrinkle appeared on her high forehead.

"Uh." I lurched forward a step, shoving my hands deep into my pockets. "Yeah, um, I was wondering if"—I cleared my throat—"Officer McKenzie was, uh, available?" My voice squeaked embarrassingly at the last word.

The smile returned to the woman's face. "I think he is, yeah." She picked up the receiver and lifted her brows at me. "Can I have your name?"

"Oh. Uh. Patrick. Patrick Bouchard."

The woman nodded and dialled, her eyes going distant as she listened to the phone ring. After a few seconds, she straightened in her chair. "Hey, Mitch? Yeah." Her cheeks dimpled as she chuckled, staring down at the desk in front of her. "No." She laughed again, *flirtatiously*. "No, that's fine. Yes, *really*."

I exhaled slowly through my nose, my jaw tight as I waited for her to tell Mitch I was there. I had considered using a fake name in case he was avoiding me on purpose but then decided the bait-and-switch would just piss him off.

"Listen, there's someone here to see you. Patrick, uh . . ." She lifted her eyes to mine, holding her hand over the receiver.

"Bouchard," I said quietly.

"Patrick Bou— Oh. Yeah. Okay. I'll tell him." She giggled again, listening, then set down the phone.

I held my breath, bracing myself to hear that he didn't want to see me.

The woman pointed to a row of moulded plastic seats next to the front door. "You can sit there if you like. He's just finishing up with something. Shouldn't be long."

"Oh thank you so much," I said in a rush, then quickly took a seat, hands clenched in front of me. *Oh my god, what am I doing?* It wasn't too late, was it? I could leave. I could leave and say that I forgot that I had something to do. I stared down at my hands—my knuckles were white. *I'm going to be sick.*

"Patrick!"

I jolted to my feet, blinking at Mitch as he approached with a wide grin.

Before I could say anything, he clapped a hand on my shoulder. "How come you didn't tell me you were stopping by?" The way Mitch said it made it sound like we were the greatest of friends.

What is happening?

He turned to the woman at the desk. "Thanks, Samira. I'll take it from here, doll." He winked and gave her a saucy grin, and she flapped her hand in his direction, rolling her eyes but obviously charmed by his absurd flirting.

"C'mon Patrick, I'll give you a tour."

"Uh. Okay. Sure." I smiled nervously.

With his hand amicably on my shoulder, Mitch steered me in the direction of the long corridor on the left, but as soon as we reached the end and turned out of sight of Samira, Mitch shifted his grip to the back of my neck and squeezed hard enough that I let out a soft yelp.

Oh no.

Without a word, Mitch pulled open an unmarked blue door and then shoved me so hard I stumbled and fell, landing in a heap against a jumble of banker's boxes half-filled with beige file folders.

"Ow," I said quietly, rubbing my shoulder where it had connected with the corner of a box. Mitch closed the door and stalked towards me, his face a mask of fury.

Oh no. He's going to kill me. Why am I so stupid? Why did I do it? I lifted my hands to shield myself. If only I could breathe, I could scream for help.

"What the *fuck* are you doing here, you goddamn piece of shit?" Mitch said in a harsh whisper. He grabbed me with both hands, hauling me to my feet, and shook me hard as he glared down at me.

I gaped up at him, trying to form words.

"I-I-I, well"—I winced as he dug his fingers into my flesh—"you didn't answer my messa—"

Mitch shook me again, making my teeth clack together, then suddenly released me. I fell back against a filing cabinet, hitting my head.

"Are you that fucking *stupid*?" he snarled, balling his fists at his sides. "Are you *really* that fucking dimwitted? Eh, shitbird? I'm talking to you. Fucking answer me."

"I'm . . . I don't—" I cowered against the filing cabinet as he stepped forward again. "I'm sorry! I'm sorry!" I said, my voice breaking. "I was *worried*."

Mitch turned the corners of his mouth down and tilted his head, leaning towards me. "I-I-I-I was w-w-w-worried," he said, pitching his voice higher, mocking me. He shook his head, giving me a withering look. "Aww. Poor sad little faggot is too stupid to take a fucking hint? Jesus Christ, Patrick. What the *fuck*?"

I hiccupped a breath, tears coursing down my cheeks as I wiped my nose with the back of my wrist. "What did I do?" I whispered, then flinched as he jabbed a finger into my sternum.

"You really are that stupid, aren't you? I fucking cut your Nancy-ass loose, and instead of counting your lucky stars that I'm not wearing out that sloppy cunt of yours anymore . . . you come to my *place of work*?" He stared at me, incredulous. "What the *fuck*, Patrick?"

My bottom lip trembled as I looked away, unable to face the utter contempt in his eyes. "I'm s-s-sorry," I said, my breath hitching in my chest as I wept, making it hard to speak. "I th-th-thought—"

"No. You didn't." He jabbed me again. "Look at me when I'm talking to you."

Trembling, I lifted my streaming eyes to his.

"You *didn't* think," he said sternly, his blue eyes narrowed. "So let me tell you how it is, since you're so fucking stupid. I don't want to see you again. I'm *done* with you. See, I've got myself a brand new fuckboy and his hole is a helluva lot tighter than that gaping cunt of yours. And he doesn't fucking *cry* all the fucking time." Mitch gave me one last sharp poke in the chest, then straightened and crossed his arms, shaking his head as I continued to sob.

I've been replaced.

It was like the world was mirrored for a split second and, on one side, there was a Patrick who was relieved that it was all over. He was getting his life back. He was free.

On the flip side, the ground opened up and swallowed the other Patrick whole, robbing him of sight and sound and breath and purpose . . . and yet I was both those Patricks at once. It was too much. I slid down to the floor, my knees like jelly.

Mitch frowned as he watched me sit there with my back against the filing cabinet, my sobs just breathy little hiccups.

"All right. Quit that. Wipe your fucking face."

I pulled the sleeves of my hoodie over my hands and used them to dry my face, but I couldn't stop the tears from running down my cheeks. "I'm sorry."

The muscles bunched in his jaw, and he shook his head again in disgust. "You're fucking pathetic."

"I know," I whispered.

Mitch's eyebrows twitched up in response, like he was surprised, then he reached down and grabbed me by the forearm, yanking me to my feet.

"Come on, dipshit. I gotta get back to work."

Numbly, I followed him back down the corridor, ducking my head to hide my tear-stained face as we passed Samira at the front desk.

"Well, it was nice seein' ya, buddy," Mitch said loudly, giving me a friendly thump on the back. "Don't be a stranger, eh?" He opened the inner glass door for me, then followed me into the little vestibule.

When I turned to see what he was doing, he leaned closer to me, fixing me with a grim glare.

"Now, if you ever fucking step foot here again, I will *beat the living tar out of you*," he said in a quiet, menacing voice. Then his expression suddenly changed, and his eyes became unfocused, like he was remembering something. He frowned, shaking his head as he turned away.

I stood there watching his broad back as he walked back into the police station.

"Poor guy's dog just died," he explained to Samira as the door closed behind him.

In a daze, I let myself out of the building.

CHAPTER 8
NOT PROUD

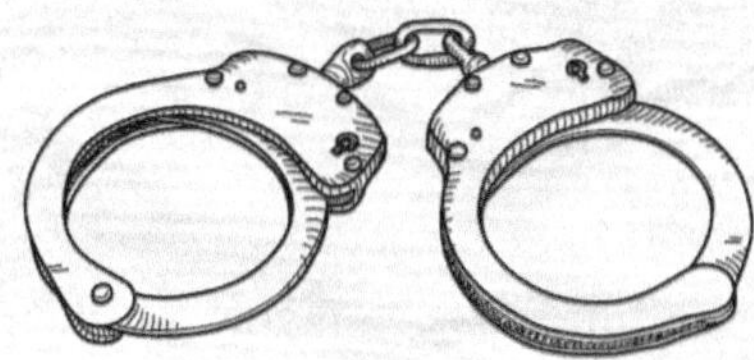

I LAY motionless in my bed in the dark, staring at nothing. The bus ride home was a blur. Strangers had asked me if I was all right every time I broke into fresh tears.

"I'm just having a bad day," I had replied mechanically to their concerns. "Thank you. I'll be okay."

Nothing felt real. It was like I had dreamed it all. Had I really gone to the police station to see Mitch? It was all very far away. Why was I so upset? I narrowed my eyes, following the streak of headlights that raced across my ceiling as a car passed outside.

Why am I like this? I had been replaced. *Why should I care?* Mitch had been so angry. And something else. I couldn't put my finger on it.

I turned to the side and stared out my bedroom window, watching the rain glint like tiny falling diamonds in the light of the streetlamp. The pillow was wet beneath my cheek.

Why am I like this? Why should I care if I've been replaced?

What's wrong with me? What did I do?

I pulled the sheet over my head and wiped my tears with it.

You don't even like Mitch. He's an asshole. He hurts you, you stupid idiot. He hurts you and hurts you and hurts you . . .

And yet he hurt me the most today.

I sighed, angry at my never-ending tears. Surely, I would run out of them eventually, and then I would pick myself up and figure out the rest of my life.

Without Mitch.

Of course, without Mitch, you dipshit. Arguing with myself was exhausting. I wished I could rewind the day. I wish I could take it back.

But then you wouldn't know you've been replaced.

I froze at a quiet sound outside my room, then pulled the sheet down, staring into the dark. There it was again. A quiet click.

There wasn't a direct line of sight from my bedroom to the front door, but the hallway suddenly brightened with the yellow glow from the entranceway light. I heard the rain clearly for a moment, and then the apartment darkened again as the front door closed with a near-silent creak. My heart was in my throat as I heard soft footfalls approaching.

Then . . . there he was, filling up my doorway, barely visible in the wan light.

Did I fall asleep? Is this a dream?

Without a word, Mitch unbuttoned his shirt and dropped it. Then he undid his belt and zipper, pulling his underwear down with his uniform pants in one motion before crawling onto the bed. I stared up at him in silence as he pulled the sheet away. Reaching over me, Mitch grabbed the bottle of lube from the bedside table, so I quickly slid down my shorts, but when I went to turn over on my stomach, as he always had me do, he touched my chest and stopped me with a little grunt and a headshake.

Mystified, I watched him lube up his cock. I gasped when he loomed over me, kneeling between my thighs, one hand on the pillow next to my head as he used the other to feed his cock slowly into my ass.

"Mm." He exhaled slowly.

I took in a quick, pained breath as his dick opened me up, and was surprised when he paused like he was giving me time to adjust instead of shoving the whole thing in like he usually did.

"It's okay," I whispered and winced when he gave me a little more.

I had no idea what to do with my arms. I was lying there like a starfish as he went down on his elbows, his furry chest brushing against me as he thrust his hips. I frowned and licked my lips, exhaling hard as his cockhead slid deeper into me.

He felt so good.

Cautiously, I lifted my hands, holding them out to either side for a moment, then slowly, *slowly*, like I was about to touch something dangerous, I placed them on Mitch's warm sides.

In response, he let out a soft moan.

Oh god. I closed my eyes and, encouraged by his apparent acceptance of my touch, I brought up my knees and wrapped my legs around his waist, pulling him into me.

"Fuck," he murmured and started fucking me faster. I slid my hands up his back, and down again, raking it gently with my nails as he drove himself into me. Precum dripped from my side to the sheets as my dick throbbed against my belly. I was already getting close. I wondered if he was too.

Moaning, I started lifting my pelvis to meet his thrusts until, eventually, I was teetered on the very edge of climax.

With a gasp, I grabbed his backside and forced him into me deep, holding him in place as the first pulse hit, his thick shaft holding me wide open as my muscles contracted. I whimpered, my hole spasming around his dick as he thrust into me hard, then let out a reedy cry as his cock swelled inside me. Mitch gave a sudden grunt, so I threw my arms around his back, panting and groaning as he quickly fucked his cum into me, his dick throbbing with every surge, filling me up as my own orgasm came to a shuddering end.

Mitch's thrusts slowed and then gradually stopped, and he rested his weight on top of me for a minute or two, his heart beating against my chest. Then, with a sigh, he rolled off of me and lay facing away.

I blinked rapidly at the ceiling, my pulse still fast and light and my head swimming with equal parts elation and confusion. I wanted to ask Mitch what had changed, but I didn't dare speak for fear of ruining whatever . . . *this* was. I glanced over, frowning.

As if he could feel my eyes boring into the back of his head, Mitch suddenly cleared his throat.

"I didn't like watching you fuck other guys," he said, his voice low and hoarse.

"What?" I asked, confused for a second. "*Oh.*"

Eyebrows high, I stayed silent for a moment, knowing better than to point out that *he* was the one who had arranged for his buddies to fuck me.

"Okay," I replied at length. *Mitch was . . . jealous? That's why he'd been so pissed off that night? Huh.*

"Don't read anything into it." Mitch glanced over his shoulder at me.

I nodded. "Okay."

He turned away from me again.

"What about . . . um . . . did you really find a new guy to—"

"There's no one else," he said gruffly. "It's just you. Now go the fuck to sleep."

I swallowed hard because it was suddenly very hard to breathe around the lump in my throat. Mitch wanted me all to himself . . . and *only* me. I felt like I was floating five feet off the bed.

Did I dare curl up to him? Put my arm around his waist? I gnawed the inside of my cheek, wondering if touching him now was pushing it. Then I remembered the last thing he'd said to me at the station and the strange pause that had followed it.

"Mitch?" I whispered, half hoping he was already asleep.

"*What?*" He sounded annoyed.

"Um. So, you said a while back that your dad used to beat the 'living tar' out of you . . ." I said timidly.

"Yeah? So?"

"You said the same sort of thing to me earlier."

Mitch remained quiet for a long time, then let out a sigh. "Yeah, I know. I sounded *just* like him."

This time, there was no pride in his voice.

CHAPTER 9
PUSHING MY LUCK

THE NEXT MORNING, I woke up to an empty bed, which wasn't unusual—Mitch never stayed over. I sighed, turning onto my back, and thought about last night.

There's no one else. It's just you. That's what he said. I could barely believe it had happened. Had I dreamt it?

I parted my thighs and reached under my balls, tilting my hips up to touch my hole. I was a little sore . . . so, *not* a dream. I smiled, thinking about how I had held onto him as he fucked me. His muscular back rolling against my palms, his furry pecs against my chest, then his backside flexing in my grasp as I came on his cock . . . I let out a low moan, squeezing my hardening shaft, and closed my eyes.

It's just you. Sure, it would have been even better if he had said something like, "You're the only one for me." But, I was happy with whatever crumbs he threw my way, fucking delusional, brain-dead idiot that I am. I started stroking myself but froze almost immediately because of a quiet squeak and then a thump from the other room.

I sat up, holding my breath as I listened hard. That squeak had sounded like my couch.

Could he . . . Did he . . .? Did I dare hope? I slid out of bed, put on my discarded boxers, and left my room, peeking around the corner.

Mitch was sitting on the couch, his feet up on the coffee table, wearing only his cop shirt, his tighty-whities, and his socks. He had a beer in one hand and the TV remote in the other and seemed to be watching a hockey game with the sound off. I noticed he hadn't combed his hair yet—it was attractively tussled.

I cleared my throat. "Hey."

"Patrick," Mitch replied by way of greeting without looking my way. He took a sip of beer as he hit the mute button on the remote, filling my apartment with the chatter of the announcer narrating the game in French. Mitch turned it down a little and set the remote aside. With his eyes still on the game, he said, "Pierre asked to switch shifts, so I have the day off."

"Ah." I scratched the back of my neck. "I was wondering why you were still here. You know, because you always go home. I mean . . . back to the motel anyway."

Mitch frowned at the television, then downed the rest of his beer as I stood there awkwardly in my boxers. I still had a partial erection, but I had my hands clasped in front of me to hide it.

"Your coffee maker is busted," Mitch said, finally glancing in my direction.

"I know."

"Here." He held his empty beer out to me. "Make yourself useful."

"Oh." I hurriedly took the bottle and went into the kitchen to fetch him a fresh one. "There you go," I said, handing it to him.

Mitch just grunted and twisted the cap off, watching the game.

I didn't know what to do or say. I was happy he was there, but he was being . . . moody. *Does he regret coming to see me last night? Should I offer to make breakfast?* As I debated sitting next to him on the couch to watch hockey, Mitch gave an audible sigh, grabbed the remote again, and killed the sound.

"I know you're *dying* to ask," he said, turning to look at me. His pale blue eyes held a challenge in them, but I had no idea what he meant.

I literally had a hundred questions to ask him—we never talked about *anything*—what did he think I wanted to know?

"Uh." I swallowed, furrowing my brow. "That's okay. You don't owe me any explanations."

"My wife kicked me out. *That's* why I'm living out of a motel."

"Ah," I said, nodding. "Okay."

He continued staring at me like he expected me to say more. Wait, was this . . . an actual *conversation*? First, he had fucked me nicely, then he stayed over, and now he wanted to *talk*? I blinked, realizing that he'd kept the TV muted earlier so that he wouldn't disturb me while I was sleeping. *What is going on here?*

"Uhh . . . so, how long ago did she kick you out?" I asked.

"Mid-May."

That was a little more than a month before Mitch found me at Parc Angrignon.

Found? You mean raped, *don't you?* I scowled inwardly, pushing the thought aside. I didn't want to ruin the pleasant moment we were having.

"You know it would be cheaper to find an apartment, right?" I said.

"Yeah, no kidding, smartass." He sighed and drank some beer. "But hey, I don't have to pick up after myself. Marisol comes in twice a week to take care of the sheets and shit like that."

"Ah." I felt an ugly twinge of jealousy, wondering if cleaning was the *only* thing this "Marisol" took care of.

No. Mitch had said *it's just you.* But . . . maybe he only meant I was the only *guy.* I thought about how he'd flirted with Samira at the police station. *Hm.*

"So . . . this wife. This is a *lady* wife? Like . . . a woman?" I couldn't help myself.

Mitch snorted. "Yes, she's a woman. I'm not a fucking fairy." He shook his head and took a swig of beer.

I scowled at him.

He smirked. "What?"

Emboldened by his taunting expression, I stepped over his legs and climbed onto the couch. Mitch's brows shot up, and he straightened, quickly pulling his feet off the coffee table as I settled down, straddling his thighs. I shifted a little forward so that his dick was nestled in the furrow of my ass—even flaccid, he had a sizeable bulge—then I cocked my head at him as I undid the top three buttons of his work shirt.

Mitch swallowed audibly, staring down at my hands.

"What are you doing?" he asked, his voice a little hoarse.

Uncovering his nipples, I pinched them gently, then rolled the hard little nubs between my fingers.

"Do you realize that when you're fucking me, you're fucking a *guy?*" I asked. His nipples weren't the only things getting hard—the bulge beneath me was quickly gaining mass.

"Hm?" Mitch looked up at me, his gaze wary.

"No matter how many times you call my ass a pussy or a cunt . . . it's *not.*" I gave his nipples another tweak, wiggling my hips to grind myself against his stiffening cock. I leaned forward to murmur in his ear. "See? Your dick is getting *so* hard because you want to fuck me, right?"

Mitch's breathing had quickened, and he made a quiet noise as I brushed my lips against the side of his neck. He smelled so good. I wanted to kiss his warm skin and taste him, but didn't want to push my luck. I pulled back to resume teasing his sensitive buds, smiling at how flushed his face was.

"I dunno . . . Call me crazy, but I think you might be attracted to guys," I said, grinning as I bit one side of my bottom lip. I arched an eyebrow.

"Stop it," Mitch whispered. The muscles bunched in his jaw,

and his nostrils quivered as he stared up at me, his expression unreadable.

"Or *what?* You're going to bust my jaw? Break my nose? Dislocate my shoulder?" I laughed quietly, rocking my pelvis backwards and forwards, rubbing myself against his hard bulge. My own dick was pushing out my shorts. "You're always threatening to hurt me, but you never *actually* go through with it." *At least not that way.* "I think maybe, just maybe . . . you *like* me." I narrowed my eyes and prodded the center of his chest playfully with my finger.

Mitch's eyes widened at my words. Then, without a word, he grabbed my finger and wrenched it hard to one side.

I heard the crack before I felt it.

I screamed and pulled my hand against my body instinctively to protect it. Tears swam in my vision as my mind reeled with pain, and I panted, clutching my wrist as I stared at Mitch in shock.

He remained expressionless, watching me suffer, but then slowly, his black brows came together over his nose. Looking confused, he pressed his lips into a tight, bloodless line.

"I . . . I don't know why I did that," he said.

"Because you're a fucking *psychopath?*" I replied, my voice uneven and shrill. The pain was beginning to radiate, a dull throbbing ache all the way down to my elbow.

"Hm." Mitch slowly exhaled, then took me by the waist, moving me gently aside. He stood. "Well. I guess I better put some pants on."

"What?" I said, blinking up at him through my tears. "You're just going to leave?"

Mitch rolled his eyes. "I'm going to drive you to the hospital, dumbass."

"Oh."

CHAPTER 10
FIXING THINGS

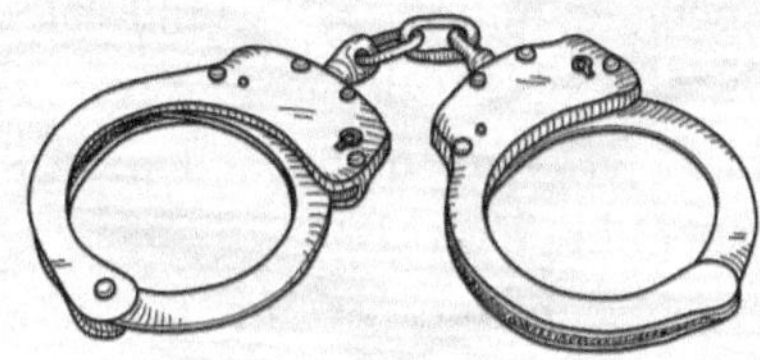

I had assumed Mitch would just drop me off, but there I was, approaching hour three in the ER waiting room, Mitch sitting next to me with an ancient *Canadian Living* magazine open in front of him.

"You really don't have to stay," I said again. "I know you've got better things to do than babysit me."

Mitch grunted and flipped the page, lifting the magazine closer to his eyes to scrutinize a pasta recipe.

"Yeah, not exactly what I pictured doing on my day off," he muttered.

Tactfully deciding not to point out that we were there *because* of him, I shifted on the moulded plastic seat and pulled out my phone again, but it was so awkward handling it left-handed that I gave up after only a few minutes. I sighed and tugged my jacket forward so it covered more of my right side. I'd had to go shirtless because nothing I owned had sleeves wide enough to pass my hand through, and my jacket was just draped over that shoulder. It was embarrassing to be bare-chested in the waiting room, not to mention a little chilly.

I gave a long sigh and then winced as the motion moved my

hand. I'd tucked it under the jacket, holding it against my chest so people would stop staring in horror at my finger jutting out at an impossible angle.

The pain was bad. It had gone from sharp to throbbing, which wasn't an improvement, and the icepack I'd brought with me had long melted. I desperately hoped they would call me soon, but I'd heard horror stories of people waiting so long to see an ER doctor that their bones had started to mend and needed to be rebroken and set before a cast could go on. *Ugh.*

Mitch echoed my sigh and sat up, frisbeeing the *Canadian Living* onto the little plastic side table before standing to peruse the selection of magazines a few rows over. He returned a few minutes later with a French-language *National Geographic* with a cowboy on the front. Settling into his seat, Mitch flipped to the main article, which, according to the cover, was *"La nouvelle conquête de L'Ouest américain,"* and went back to ignoring me.

I checked my phone and saw that we'd hit the three-hour mark. My stomach growled and I winced, shifting again in the uncomfortable seat. Did I dare go get something to eat? I looked over at Mitch. His dark brows nearly met over his nose as he read, and his lips moved ever so slightly. As I was trying to decide whether to ask Mitch if he'd get me something from the vending machine we'd passed on the way in, I heard my name.

"Patrick Bouchard?" the woman repeated as I stood. She looked up from the blue folder in her hand and glanced around.

"Oui! Ici!" I called out, holding my jacket closed as I walked up to her.

The woman smiled at me. "Follow me," she said in Haitian-accented French. She took a step and then paused, looking over my shoulder. "Your father can come in with you if you like."

I blinked at her and glanced back at Mitch across the waiting room. He just gave me a curt nod and went back to his magazine. I gave an awkward chuckle.

"No, that's okay," I said to the woman with the folder, falling in step with her as she took us down the corridor. "And he's not my father."

"Ah?" She turned to me, her brows high. "*Ah.*" Something in my expression must have tipped her off because her smile widened, dimpling her cheeks. "*Eh bien.*"

My face felt hot.

"A *very* handsome man," she said brightly in French, obviously trying to put me at ease.

"Yeah, he's not bad," I replied with a grin.

The woman laughed as she led me into a room with a large machine at its centre, which I assumed was an X-ray machine.

"It's your right hand?" she asked, looking in the folder.

"Yup." I pulled my mangled hand out from under my jacket.

"Oof." She pressed her lips together, giving me a sympathetic smile as she ran a hand over her close-cropped curls. "That looks bad. Come."

She first put an apron around my waist, explaining it was to protect me from the radiation, then had me sit down with my hand on the flat part of the machine. I gritted my teeth as she gently moved my non-damaged fingers into a better position, embarrassed by the tears that blurred my vision. She squeezed my shoulder.

"Don't worry. We'll make it all better," she said, putting a small blocky R on the table next to my hand. "Now . . . hold very still."

She left the room for only a moment and came back with a smile. "All done."

"That's it?"

"That's it." She removed the apron and gestured for me to follow her again, eventually dropping me off in a small room. She pulled fresh paper over the examination table and touched my shoulder again in a friendly way. "Good luck!"

"Thank you," I replied, then gingerly eased myself onto the table, the paper crinkling as I sat down to wait. I pulled out my phone and saw a message from Mitch:

So?

I clumsily tapped out a reply:

> x-ray done. waiting to see doc. u can go. might
> be long . . .

I waited and then smiled when his reply came back:

Don't be a fucking dumbass. I'll be here.

I jerked out of my pain-and-boredom-induced trance when the door opened about an hour later. An older man wearing a dark blue doctor's coat and matching Crocs rushed into the room, followed by a tall, bearded South Asian guy in colourful scrubs.

"Hi, Patrick," the doctor said briskly in English, holding my X-ray in one hand and a mug covered in cartoon cats in the other. His hair was a wispy arc of grey around a high, shiny forehead, and he wore his half-rim glasses so far down his long, skinny nose that I was amazed they stayed in place. "Sorry for the wait. We're slammed." He held the X-ray above his head so he could use the overhead light to read it. "So, yeah, looks like a non-complex MCP dislocation of the index with a tiny hairline fracture in the proximal."

"Oh?" I waited for him to explain, but he just handed the X-ray to the other guy before taking a sip from his mug.

"I'll let Vijay take care of you. You're in good hands," he said, patting the other man on the shoulder as he turned to leave. "Oh." The doctor frowned and dug into the pocket of his coat, pulling out a few blister packs of pills. He fanned them out between his fingers and peered at them through his glasses by craning his head back. He lifted his eyes to mine.

"Allergies?"

"Nope."

"Alrighty, then." He smiled and tossed one sheet of pills into my lap, dumping the rest back into his pocket. "Take one soon. Take the next four hours later. Probably won't need them all . . . but you never know," he said, walking away. "Good luck," he called over his shoulder and disappeared out the door.

The bearded guy grinned and shut the door. "Hi. I'm Dr. Mansukhani. Let's take a look at that finger, eh?"

"Okay," I said with a shy smile.

Dr. Mansukhani had warm, dark-amber eyes and such an easygoing vibe that I felt myself instantly start to relax. He couldn't have been more than a few years older than me and was *extremely* attractive. I watched him silently as he stuck the X-ray on a wall-mounted lightbox and leaned in to consult it.

"Normally, this would be digital, but Katz is an old-school holdout," he explained as he opened a drawer to rifle through it. "That's fine, though. I don't mind. And it's good practice to work with printed X-rays—I'm planning on volunteering with *Médecins Sans Frontières* once I'm done my residency here, and you never know what sort of equipment you'll be working with."

"Oh? That's interesting," I replied. "I've heard of them." I stared nervously at the weird metal object and blue Velcro tape he placed on the table next to me. "Aren't you going to put a cast on me?"

"For a dislocation and a teeny tiny fracture? Nah," Dr. Mansukhani said with a chuckle. "We'll just splint it."

"Oh, okay." I winced as he turned my hand over. My knuckle was super swollen and bruised. "So . . . you're, uh, going to do this sort of stuff for *Médecins Sans Frontières*, then?" I asked, trying to distract myself from both the pain and the handsome doctor's proximity. His touch was giving me little shivers.

"I'm actually going to be an orthopaedic surgeon. Katz just has me doing grunt work like this because I have a knack for it." He looked up from my hand and gave me a wry grin. "Not that I mind it."

I got the impression that very little bothered Dr. Mansukhani.

After a beat, he went back to inspecting my knuckle and dislocated finger. "You have very nice hands, by the way. Structurally speaking."

I felt the flush creep up my neck. Was he . . . flirting with me? It seemed like it.

See? This is the kind of guy you should be with! My inner voice screamed at me. *Closer to your age. Kind-hearted. Smart. And he's a doctor!* I clenched my jaw. *Not a shitty rapist cop who hurts and uses you and treats you like crap.*

My phone buzzed in my lap, and I opened my eyes to see a message from Mitch. *His ears must have been burning.*

> ETA?

I sighed.

"My uhhh . . ." My brain stalled, not sure what word to use to describe Mitch. "My friend wants to know how much longer I'm going to be. He's my lift."

"Oh! Not long at all," Dr. Mansukhani said, sitting up on his wheeled stool. "So . . . are you ready?"

"Oh god," I whispered. "Okay. Hang on." I slowly typed out my message:

> not long now.

Mitch responded right away:

> K

I put my phone back in my pocket and grimaced. "All right. I'm ready."

Dr. Mansukhani gave me a sympathetic smile and nodded. "I promise I'll make it as quick as I can."

It was quick . . . but in no way painless.

CHAPTER 11
GOOD PILLS

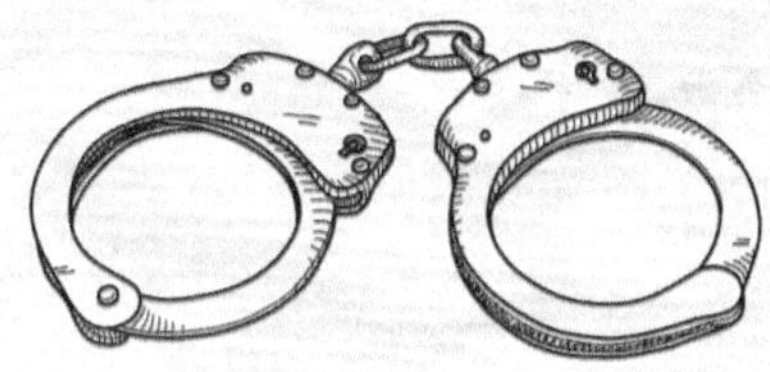

STILL REELING from Dr. Mansukhani resetting and splinting my finger, I walked across the waiting room in a daze. Mitch was still where I had left him, but now he had his arms folded, hands tucked under his biceps, with his chin against his chest and legs outstretched in front of him, crossed at the ankles. Apparently, he'd decided to take a nap.

I nudged the sole of his boot gently. "Hey."

Slowly, Mitch raised his head and blinked up at me, his gaze unfocused for a moment.

"About fucking time," he said, then yawned, sitting up. "Jesus, did they build you a whole new hand?"

"Dislocated fingers are sorta low priority," I replied with a shrug.

"Hm." Mitch yawned again and grabbed his jacket as he stood. "All right. Let's get the hell out of here."

I followed him but paused to grab a bottle of water from the vending machine on our way out so that I could swallow one of the pills Dr. Katz had given me. I got into the passenger seat of Mitch's car, careful not to bang my wrapped hand on anything, and then sat mutely as he circled the hospital parking lot to get to the barrier gate at the exit.

"Um. Thanks for the lift. And waiting for me," I said into the awkward silence.

Mitch just grunted and nodded, then leaned out the window to scan the parking pass.

The barrier lifted, and as we turned onto the main road, my stomach rumbled loudly. I made a face.

"Sorry," I said.

"Hungry?"

I glanced over. "Uh, yeah, actually." Between all the pain and the stress, I'd completely forgotten that I hadn't eaten all day.

Without a word, Mitch made a slow U-turn and passed the hospital again, going east for a few blocks before heading north. I smiled as we pulled up to the little deli near Decarie Boulevard. They made some of the best smoked meat sandwiches in town, in my opinion.

"Be right back," Mitch said, putting on his hazards. He got out, slammed the door hard, and left me double-parked out in front. The music playing on the car stereo started immediately cutting out as Mitch's cheap Bluetooth adapter struggled to stay connected to his phone—I waited until he was out of sight so he didn't see me touching his stereo and pressed the button to switch from AUX to the radio.

The dial was set to CHOM, which played classic and hard rock—not really my thing. However, it was better than some of the screaming weirdness in Mitch's regular playlists—he listened almost exclusively to bands from the eighties and nineties with charming names like Skinny Puppy, Nine Inch Nails, and Tool.

I frowned at the radio music coming from the Corolla's shitty speakers.

Ugh. Nickelback.

I squinted at the shop window, trying to see how busy the deli was so I could gauge how long Mitch would be, and then I shrugged to myself. *Whatever.* Feeling unusually daring, I turned the radio knob until I found some Dua Lipa. I smiled and sat back, studying the Velcro tape holding the metal splint to my finger. I probably needed to wear it for six weeks, but I had been given an appointment with Dr. Katz at his main practice, halfway across the island, in four weeks to see how it was healing. In the meantime, I was supposed to tighten the tape as the swelling went down. I tried wiggling my finger in the splint.

Huh. The pain in my hand had diminished dramatically. *Good pills.*

The door of the Corolla creaked open, startling me, and Mitch tossed a butcher-paper-wrapped sandwich in my lap before settling himself behind the wheel. He quickly tore the paper from his smoked meat sandwich and then paused as he went to take a bite. Mitch slowly shifted his gaze from his sandwich to the car stereo and stared at it for a few long seconds as Billie Eilish came on. Locking his pale blue gaze on me, he turned the dial back to CHOM.

I let out a nervous chuckle. "Sorry."

Mitch shook his head, then bit into his sandwich, keying the engine as he chewed. The Corolla sputtered to life, and he threw it into Drive, steering one-handed as he ate.

Unwrapping my sandwich with my injury proved to be difficult, but I got there in the end. I took up half the sandwich, balancing the other on the paper in my lap, and took a bite. My forehead wrinkled up in surprise.

"You got mine with Swiss cheese and that crunchy, spicy mustard?"

"Well, that's the way you fucking like it, isn't it?" Mitch said gruffly as he did a shoulder check, quickly changing lanes.

I beamed. "You remembered."

"Just eat your fucking sandwich."

I munched happily as we sped down the street. I wondered if the deli had changed something about the sandwich because it was the best one I'd ever eaten—*so* good. I chuckled to myself. Maybe it was just that Mitch had gotten it made special for me.

I ate in silence for a few minutes when something occurred to me.

"Hey, how come you don't have a partner?" I asked.

"What?"

"You know. A cop buddy? A sidekick?" I frowned as the buildings flying by the Corolla started looking streaky and blurred. I shook my head and blinked hard. "I thought cops were supposed to have partners."

"Oh." Mitch darted onto the bike path to pass the next car. "Well, I pair up with Tank sometimes."

"Tank?" I laughed. "Is that his real name?"

Mitch snorted and rolled his eyes. "What do you think, dumbass? His name is Tankian. Can never remember his first name. He's an Armenian . . . built like a brick shithouse. Quiet as a mouse. We get along."

"Why only 'sometimes'?"

Mitch frowned, his eyes on the road ahead. "Uh, we get along *most* of the time."

"I meant, why don't you have a partner *all* of the time?"

"Oh." Mitch shrugged. "Dunno."

"Maybe it's because of your sparkling personality." Mitch shot me another glance, and I snickered, shaking my head before taking another bite. *So good.*

"Just shut up and eat, will ya?"

A few seconds later, we screeched to a halt at a red light, and Mitch sighed, waited a few seconds, then reached down . . . only to frown and quickly put his hand back on the steering wheel.

"Ha! Oh my god, you are *so* fucking impatient."

Mitch looked over at me with his brow furrowed. "What's that?"

"You just went to turn on your siren," I said, grinning. "You thought we were in your police car."

"I don't know what the fuck you're talking about."

I snorted. "I totally saw you."

"Yeah, whatever." He went back to staring at the red light, popping the last bite of his sandwich into his mouth before crumpling the paper into a ball and throwing it over his shoulder into the back seat.

"Want me to lean out the window and make siren noises?" I asked, giggling. "Woop! Woop! Bee-woop! *Weeeeeooooooooooo*—"

"Will you shut the *fuck* up?" Mitch said, glaring at me. "The fuck is wrong with you?"

I laughed again, this time a little uneasily. "Uhh. I dunno." I felt lightheaded and . . . tingly.

The car behind us honked, and Mitch stepped on the gas, flooring it as we crossed the intersection.

"Honk at me? Fuck you, you fucking fucker," Mitch said under his breath as he wove through traffic.

It felt like we were going *way* too fast—I realized I was getting a little queasy. I burped, and the feeling passed, but the weirdness in my head was only getting worse. Plus, my skin was vibrating.

"Oh," I said. "Oh shit. I think I'm *stoned*."

Mitch snickered, shooting an amused glance at me before he took a sharp corner.

"That so?"

"Yeah, I think the drugs just really kickled in." I burst out laughing. "Kickled? I mean kicked."

"Oh boy," Mitch said with a smirk, shaking his head again.

I stared down at my half-eaten sandwich—my nausea was returning.

"I don't feel so great."

"Don't you puke in my fucking car."

"Um. Okay."

Mitch glanced over at me, his brow deeply creased.

"Should I pull over? D'you want me to pull over?"

I burped again and thumped my chest. "Uh. No. No, I think

I'm okay. Maybe? But I'm gonna save this for later," I replied, re-wrapping my sandwich.

"All right. Yeah," Mitch said, pushing the Corolla to go even faster, "we're almost home anyway."

I laughed.

"What?" Mitch's eyes darted to the side.

"You just called my apartment 'home.' "

"I meant *your* home, dipshit," he replied. He then rolled down the passenger window and the cold fall air blasted me in the face. "Here, breathe deep. It'll help."

I nodded. I started feeling better almost immediately, and by the time we pulled up to my apartment, I no longer felt sick. *Definitely* still stoned, but it was a nice mellow high.

Mitch put the Corolla in Park. After watching me struggle with the passenger-side door for a few seconds, he sighed and got out of the car. He went around and yanked the door open.

"C'mon. Get out."

I set my sandwich down on the center console and then fumbled with the seatbelt for a while before Mitch finally leaned over me to undo it.

"Thanks." I swivelled in the seat, put my feet on the sidewalk and . . . nothing happened.

"Patrick?"

I looked up at Mitch. "Uh. I don't know if my legs'll work."

Mitch rolled his eyes. "Jesus." He stared up at the sky, his jaw clenched. For a moment, I thought he was angry, but then he let out a long sigh that ended with a chuckle. "How are you feeling otherwise? Still nauseous?"

"Nope."

"Okay, good." He reached down and grabbed my left wrist, and before I knew what was happening, he had slung me over his shoulder like a sack of potatoes.

"Hey!" I clutched his waist as he swung around and slammed the car door shut. I hung there helplessly as he climbed the front steps to my apartment and let himself in with his keys. Then he went straight to my room, where he dropped me on the bed.

"God, you're such a caveman," I said, laughing.

"Am I?" Mitch sat on the edge of the bed and leaned over me, his eyes narrowed, looking amused.

"Totally. You've got the whole 'alphahole' thing down."

"The what now?"

I smiled but decided not to explain. I didn't want him to get insulted. He was being nice to me again, whether out of guilt for busting my finger—though he had yet to apologize—or just because he was in a good mood, I wasn't sure, but I was enjoying it.

"You know, the X-ray tech thought you were my dad."

Mitch snorted. "I'm not that old."

"Okay, Boomer. Whatever you wanna believe," I said, teasing.

"Hey!" He grinned, prodding me in the ribs. "I'm Gen X, asshole."

"*Exactly.* Old enough to be my dad," I replied, trying to bat his hand away.

"Really?" Mitch stopped tickling me, his eyebrows high.

"Well, yeah." I wrinkled my nose at him, biting the corner of my bottom lip as I gave him a coy smile. "Maybe I should start calling you 'Daddy' from now on."

The change in his expression was instantaneous. He grabbed my wrist and pinned it to the bed next to my head, leaning down closer to me, his features contorted in fury.

"Don't you fucking call me that," he said in a hoarse, barely controlled voice. A vein throbbed in his forehead as he stared at me wide-eyed. "*Never.*"

I knew then in my gut, without a shadow of a doubt, that the man who had broken Mitch's arm had done far worse to him . . . and my heart ached for that little boy who just wanted to dance to David Bowie.

I reached up with my wounded hand and cupped the back of Mitch's head, pulling him down to me quickly before he had a chance to react. At first, his lips were a hard, unyielding line—but that didn't stop me. He wasn't pulling away, so I kissed him more insistently, his stubble scraping my lips as I held onto him. Then, suddenly, he relented, opening up to me with a strangled moan.

Mitch's tongue met mine with an eagerness that surprised me, and as he leaned his weight on me, he slipped a hand under my neck, squeezing my nape, and his mouth moved over mine with such fervour that I felt like I was being devoured.

I whimpered into the fervid kiss, breathless and aching as he rolled on top of me, grinding his hardening cock between my legs until, finally, I wrenched my head away from him with a gasp.

"Oh *fuck*," I rasped, my chest heaving as I desperately tried to pull air into my lungs.

Eyes heavy-lidded, Mitch stared down at me for only a moment, then lunged forward again to recapture my mouth. It was surprising and intoxicating the way he poured his desire into the kiss, his repressed passion bruising my lips and stealing my breath until I began to worry I would pass out—but then, abruptly, Mitch pulled away.

His eyes were closed, and a deep wrinkle slowly formed between his dark brows as he panted softly above me.

Uh oh.

Before he could retreat back into himself and shut me out again, I shifted my pelvis up and grabbed his ass with my good hand, pressing him down against me.

"Mitch . . . I want you inside me," I murmured.

Mitch's eyes popped open as a small groan escaped from between his reddened lips. He quickly went up on his knees, resting on his haunches as he wrestled my jeans and boxers down, then he parted my thighs and undid his pants, only lowering them enough that he could pull out his cock. He spat twice in his palm, wet his dick, and came forward again, sinking himself into my splayed hole with a grunt. It hurt . . . but it was a pain I welcomed.

"Oh fuck, *yes*. You feel so good." I clutched at him, encouraging him to go deeper as he shuddered in pleasure, his thick cock opening me up as I sought out his mouth again.

Mitch growled, attacking my tongue with his as he began frantically pumping his hips, his dick going fully crown to root every time he drove himself into me hard. There was a desperate edge to his furious thrusts, something I'd never felt from him before.

Soon, I was moaning with every plunge, my voice growing louder as my looming orgasm began gathering speed, and when I pulled away from Mitch's fierce kiss, it was to let out a hoarse, unhinged shout.

As my cock erupted, Mitch matched my cry and came with me, his dick twitching and swelling in time to the waves of pleasure that rippled my hole over the thick, cum-covered shaft buried to the balls inside me. Then he let out a few deep grunts, the gasps in between nearly as loud, and whimpered before he collapsed onto me, shivering as he buried his face in my neck.

I lay there, fighting to catch my breath as I stroked Mitch's back, my sensitive hole still pulsating around his spent dick, giving me shivers.

"Wow," I said quietly. "That was amazing."

At the sound of my voice, Mitch stiffened and pushed himself off and out of me, shifting to sit farther away on the edge of the bed. He stared forward with a strange, subdued expression for a few long seconds, then rubbed a hand over his mouth.

"Mitch?" When he didn't respond, I reached for his arm, but he flinched. "What's wrong?"

"Nothing," Mitch muttered and stood. He swore softly under his breath when he saw that my cum had gotten all over the front of his T-shirt and pants. Sighing, he ran a hand through his hair. He turned to me, but when our eyes met, he quickly looked to the side. "Um." The muscles worked in his jaw, and to my surprise, a slight flush crept up his neck as he stood there looking dazed and uncertain. It was like he was a different person . . . but it only lasted a moment. Mitch cleared his throat and swallowed, his shoulders visibly squaring as his expression hardened to its usual smug detachment.

"Yeah, it was all right," he said with a dismissive shrug and a smile, meeting my gaze.

I frowned at him. "Don't do that."

"Do what?"

"Act like you're incapable of feeling anything."

Mitch's brow furrowed, and he started to respond but faltered, looking a little lost for a few seconds. His nostrils flared, and he dropped his eyes, staring at nothing for a few beats. Then, he shook his head, took a deep breath, and locked eyes with me.

"I don't know what you want me to say, Patrick."

I blinked at him for several seconds, then sighed when nothing came to me.

"You know what? I don't know either."

Mitch smirked. "Well, that settles *that*, then."

But he had used my name. Not "sunshine" or "kid" or even his favourite, "dipshit." *And* he'd sounded earnest. *I'll take it.*

Glancing back down at the mess on his clothes, Mitch tucked his limp cock back into his pants to zip up.

"I guess I gotta go get changed."

I perked up. "Does that mean you're coming back here after?"

"Uh." He frowned at me. "I mean . . . do you want me to?"

I nodded.

"Fine," Mitch replied in a gruff voice and left.

I touched my bruised lips and smiled.

CHAPTER 12
TRAPPED

Mitch was gone when I woke up the next morning. We hadn't exactly cuddled during the night, but after he'd fucked me a second time, he hadn't moved away, and we had lain there with our shoulders touching until I fell asleep.

It was . . . something.

I winced, massaging my forearm where the pain from my injury was radiating and sighed. Was I really so stupid as to believe that somehow Mitch would change and become . . . what? My boyfriend? I shook my head as I walked through my empty apartment to the bathroom to relieve myself.

Did I even *like* him? I couldn't tell. I craved his affection and his attention like nothing else . . . but was it all just some sort of Stockholm-esque thing I was going through? I shook my head. Instead of thinking about the handsome doctor from yesterday, I was hunting desperately for any tiny hint that Mitch might actually like me.

You're dreaming.

Then how do you explain last night? He was downright nice to me. I pointed out to my inner critic.

In my distraction, I forgot I was wearing a splint and hit the side of the toilet as I went to flush. I yelped and clung to my wrist as I waited for the pain to recede.

Fuck it. I popped another of Dr. Katz's killer pills from the pack and washed it down. Mitch was probably at work, and I didn't start my shift until three. I'd get blitzed on pain meds, sleep until noon, get up and maybe order pizza . . . and then play some *Genshin Impact* before work. I frowned, looking down at my hand. *Hm.* I wasn't sure how well I could play with my finger busted, but I was sure I could switch some controls around. I shrugged to myself and smiled. *Whatever.* Whether it was *Genshin* or a movie, it was going to be a nice, relaxing afternoon.

I woke up with a start, my heart pounding as the last of the nightmare melted away from my consciousness. Something about . . . falling into a pit? I sat up and rubbed my face, then glanced over at the clock. It was nearly two—no wonder I felt so groggy. And *hungry.*

I dragged myself out of bed, threw on some jeans and a hoodie, and went to the kitchen to fix myself something to eat. I settled on cereal, but the milk had gone bad, so I had to make do with water. I was also out of juice, so I grabbed the last beer from the fridge. I tucked the bottle under my arm and started eating my watery cereal, but stopped mid-chew when I saw my apartment lease sitting on the dining table.

Swallowing my off-brand Froot Loops, I set down my breakfast and picked up the lease, wondering why Mitch was going through my stuff . . . and immediately realized that it was a *new* lease for my apartment.

Huh. I blinked a few times in confusion, staring at the name written in the tenant section: Mitch McKenzie. I flipped through the pages—my name was nowhere to be found. *What the fuck?*

Taking it with me to the couch, I sat down in a daze as I finished my cereal. I kept picking the lease up to check the address again, thinking I'd misread it and Mitch was moving in next door, but no, that was *my* address. And, for some reason, the rent had gone down by fifty bucks. I drank down the beer too quickly, giving myself a buzz, and wished I had more to help me deal with this . . . fuckery.

I got up to get my phone from the bedroom to ask Mitch what the *fuck* was going on and was startled when the front door suddenly opened.

Mitch came into the apartment carrying a big cardboard box and kicked the door shut behind him before dropping the box on the floor. It looked like it was full of clothes.

"Oh look who's finally decided to get his lazy ass out of bed." He smirked.

"What the fuck is *this*?" I asked, holding up the lease.

Mitch frowned. "It's a lease, dumbass."

"Yes, I know it's a fucking lease. But why does it have your name on it?"

"Because I'm moving in," he said evenly, hooking his thumbs in his belt as he stared down at me.

"Why isn't *my* name on the lease?"

Shrugging, Mitch twisted his mouth to the side dismissively before answering. "I figured it just made more sense this way."

"What? *Why?*"

"Listen, I thought this was what you wanted."

I did. He was right . . . but not like *this*. "When did I say that?" I asked, my voice a little hoarse from trying to rein in my anger. The beer had definitely gotten to my head.

"You kept saying it was cheaper to get an apartment than live at the motel . . . you know, and asking me to stay over." He shrugged again. This time, he looked a little less sure of himself. "So what the fuck is the problem?"

"The problem is that you've apparently *stolen* my apartment."

"Stolen?" Mitch laughed. "Listen, kid, it just made sense for me to be the one footing the bill. I've got the money and I'm a helluva lot more responsible than you are."

"How's that?" I clenched my jaw as I glared up at him.

"Your landlord says you've been late with rent four times—"

"Three times. It was *three* times," I said.

"Well, he said *four*."

"Well, he's lying."

"Regardless," Mitch said, shaking his head condescendingly, "you've been late. And just look at you." He pointed to my hoodie. "When was the last time you washed your fucking clothes?"

I looked down and saw there was a dried stain on the front. I rubbed it self-consciously.

"What does that have to do with anything?"

"Your place is a fucking pigsty, you eat like shit, and you don't take care of yourself. I thought faggots were supposed to be all neat and tidy. What happened with you?"

"I guess I missed the fucking memo," I snapped back.

Mitch sneered. "Well, now that this is *my* place, things are going to fucking change, aren't they?"

I let out a groan of frustration. "It's still my apartment! I don't know how you got Mr. Faucher to change the lease, but it can't be legal. What did you do? Go to his place and intimidate him with your police bullshit?" Mitch was in uniform but without his hat and vest. "Did you bully him into signing it over?"

"No. In fact, he gave me a fucking *discount* because he fucking *likes* that he's going to have a fucking *cop* around."

"Whatever. It is *bull*shit." I ripped the lease in half and dropped it on the floor. "And I don't have time for it." I glanced at the clock on the microwave. "I have to get to work."

"Pick that up." Mitch pointed to the torn papers. "And, no. You don't. Not anymore." He sounded smug.

Alarmed, I stared at him for a few beats. "What did you do?" I asked slowly.

"I told your boss that you're finished working there."

"You *what?*" I clenched my fists and winced as the motion pulled on my wounded finger. "*Why* would you do that?"

"Because, Patrick, it's a dead-end fucking job. And you don't need it anyway, seeing as I'm the one paying for rent now."

"Jesus fuck." I was so outraged I was shaking.

"This way, you can get your shit together and go back to school and finish your fucking Engineering degree."

"*What?* There's no way in hell I'm going back . . . I dropped out because I fucking *hated* it. I told you that."

"So you took out all that loan money for nothing then?" Mitch raised his eyebrows. "Not very *responsible* of you."

"Oh my god," I replied, looking up at the ceiling as I took a few deep breaths.

"Okay. Don't go back to Engineering . . . but you're going to go back to school to do *something* with yourself. Don't like university? Fine. You can go to trade school. At least you'll be doing something with yourself that isn't sitting around in dirty clothes and jerking off to video games."

I barked out a laugh, staring at him in stunned disbelief. The fucking *balls* on him . . .

"And, I suppose you're going to pay my way too?" I narrowed my eyes at him. "Since I don't have any money of my own anymore?"

"Yes. And I'm going to make sure you're *not* going to waste my money."

"You forgot to add 'young man' to that," I said quietly.

Mitch's brows came together.

"You know . . ." I made my voice deeper and shook my finger at him. "Don't waste my money, *young man*." Snorting, I shook my head. "If you don't *want* me to call you 'Daddy,' why the *fuck* are you trying so hard to be my father, huh?"

The way Mitch's eyes went suddenly cold should have rung alarm bells, but I was too pissed off to care.

"Except, *my* father would never bully me or abuse me or try to control my life," I continued, curling my lip at him. "And he certainly would never *fuck* me . . . Oh wait, that's *your* father." As soon as the words left my lips, I knew I had gone too far. *Way* too far.

Mitch grabbed me by the throat and shoved me backwards. I stumbled against the dining table and then landed hard on my ass, knocking the wind out of me. I was unable to breathe for a few terrifying seconds but finally sucked in some air when Mitch hauled me to my feet. I coughed and yelped as he swung me around, pushing me down onto the freestanding counter that separated the kitchen and living room. Leaning all his weight on me, Mitch grabbed my arm and slung it down over the other side of the counter, wrenching my shoulder in the process. I heard a jingle and realized what was happening only as cold metal touched my wrist. Twisting my hand, I tried to evade the handcuff, but he secured it with a ratcheting *clink*, locking the other end of it through the metal pull handle on the cupboard door below.

Satisfied that I was restrained, he yanked down hard on my jeans only to find they wouldn't budge—I'd lost so much weight that my favourite jeans wouldn't stay up without a belt. With an angry growl, Mitch tried to reach my buckle to undo my pants, but it was trapped under me. I craned my neck to look at him and was terrified by the fury on Mitch's face.

"I'm sorry," I said, the tears welling up. "I'm sorry, Mitch. I had a beer. It got to my head. I'm sorry."

Without a word, he grabbed the seat of my pants, and I heard a sawing noise followed by a loud *rip*. When cool air touched my ass, I realized that he'd used a knife to slice through my jeans and boxers before tearing them open with his fingers. I whimpered, turning away to press my forehead to the cold countertop as his heavy cop belt hit the floor.

Oh god. Oh god.

I screamed as his cock split me open, then wheezed in pain as he started fucking me through the hole in my jeans. Mitch forced himself deep as I sobbed, taking his rage out on me one vicious thrust at a time, then I groaned in despair as the inevitable began to happen.

My dick was trapped in a twist of my boxers and was squashed between my pelvis and the countertop, so it hardened into the most painfully uncomfortable boner I'd ever experienced. I gasped as Mitch started fucking me faster, ramming me against the counter so hard I knew I'd be bruised, then I crushed my eyes closed with a moan.

"Oh *fuck*," I whispered as the pressure mounted inside me, my hole clamping tight around the thick base of Mitch's cock.

Mitch suddenly grunted, pounding into me as he blew his load, his cum-slick cock launching me into the throes of orgasm as he rooted himself deep.

I wailed, my thighs trembling as I filled the front of my shorts and drowned my aching, bent erection in cum. I could barely breathe as every clenching contraction built on the previous until I was just a quivering, weeping mess.

Panting, Mitch pulled out. I heard the rustle of cloth and blearily twisted my neck to see what he was doing. He'd zipped himself back up and was buckling his belt, his cheeks ruddy from exertion and forehead beaded with sweat as he met my gaze.

Mitch turned away from me and grabbed his keys off the countertop.

"Going to the gym," he muttered.

"Wait!" I called after him, but he didn't stop. "Mitch?" The door slammed after him, and I let out a whimper. Cum ran slowly down my inner thigh as I bowed my head and cried.

· · ·

By the time I heard Mitch's boots on the front stairs, it was past nine. I was cold, uncomfortable, and miserable, but at least I'd managed to crawl over the counter to sit on the floor in the kitchen instead of spending six hours on my stomach. Still, my wrist hurt from being cuffed for so long, and my ass was numb from sitting on the hard tiles.

The door swung open, and Mitch walked in. A moment later, he clicked on the kitchen light, blinding me. I shielded my eyes, blinking rapidly as Mitch stared down at me. He had a hazy, amused look on his face, and from the way he swayed a little as he stood there, I realized he was drunk.

"S'that piss?" he asked, grinning as he pointed to the takeaway soup container on the floor.

"What else was I going to do? Piss on the floor?" I replied angrily.

Mitch just snickered and shrugged, then went to turn the light back off.

"Gonna hit th'sack."

"Hey!" I shouted, alarmed. "Aren't you forgetting something?"

Turning back to me, Mitch furrowed his brow, looking bemused.

I jingled the handcuffs. "The key?"

"Oh, right." He dug into his pocket and tossed the handcuff key in my lap. Then he turned off the light, plunging the kitchen back into darkness, and shuffled off to the bedroom.

I awkwardly unlocked the handcuff with my wounded hand and sighed with relief, massaging my wrist for a moment before attempting to get to my feet. Grimacing, I forced my aching legs to bend and then stood, clutching the countertop until the tingling finally stopped. With a sigh, I turned the light back on and picked up the bowl of piss, rinsing it out in the sink before dumping it in the recycling bin alongside the empty box of crackers that had been my supper. Then, I cleaned the dried cum off the floor and sopped up the spilled vegetable oil that Mitch had evidently used on me as lube earlier.

Once the kitchen was sorted out, I stripped naked, threw my torn jeans and boxers in the trash, and got in the shower. The warm water washed my tears away as I quickly soaped myself up, being extra gentle with my sore, swollen hole. Once I was done, I stood in the hallway in my towel, staring at the couch in the living room.

Who am I kidding?

Shoulders slumped, I went quietly into my room and groped around in the dark until I found my dresser. After slipping on a fresh pair of boxers, I eased myself into bed next to Mitch, being careful not to wake him.

Mitch snorted, then snored louder for a few breaths, absolutely reeking of whiskey, then fell silent.

I checked my phone and saw that he had messaged me twice—once, about an hour after he'd left, asking me to make supper; then, two hours later, the message just said, "nvm."

"Why didn't you just take the handle off the cupboard?" Mitch said, startling me.

"What?" I frowned. "Uh . . . how was I supposed to do that?"

"With a screwdriver, dumbass," Mitch replied with a chuckle.

I *was* a dumbass. *Fuck*, he was right. There had been a screwdriver within reach the whole time in the kitchen junk drawer.

"Oh my god." I sighed.

Mitch laughed again. "That way, you wouldn't have had to pee in the Tupperware."

I ignored him and turned onto my side, facing away from him.

"C'mere." Mitch grabbed me by the hip, sliding me backwards. He pushed his pelvis against my ass, and I immediately shoved him away—he was naked and his dick was hard.

"No. Fuck off," I said, regretting my decision not to sleep on the couch.

Mitch hooked his fingers into the waistband of my boxers and pulled them down before I could stop him, and when I tried to roll over onto my back, he quickly slid his arm between my neck and pillow and wrapped his arm around my chest, holding me tightly against him as he fumbled at my ass with the other hand.

"I said *no*. Mitch . . . Mitch, stop it!" I said, struggling as he poked around at my ass crack with his dick. I kicked my heel back against his legs, but unfortunately, that gave him leverage to pry my thighs apart with his knee. I gasped in pain, thrashing in his arms as he tried unsuccessfully to get his cock into me without lube.

Panting, I tried to wiggle free when he shifted to grab the bottle on the nightstand, but he was too strong, and my nails were too short to do any real damage to his forearm.

I heard the squirt of lube and frantically started shifting my pelvis from side to side, trying to evade his dick.

"Jesus," Mitch muttered, pinning my leg down with his knee to hinder my movements. "Stop . . . *huhh* . . . fighting me, Patrick."

"Stop. Stop it. *Stop* it," I said, my voice hoarse as his slippery cockhead made contact with my sore hole again. I closed my eyes and let out a strangled wail as he successfully pushed himself into me, splitting me open as he sank himself deep.

Mitch draped his arm around my waist, thrusting slowly a few times . . . and then he stopped.

"There," he said softly. "That's all I wanted."

I opened my eyes, confused. My hole clenched involuntarily, and his dick twitched in response, but he just lay there, not moving. He then touched the back of my head with his face. The second and third time he did it, I realized they were kisses.

What the . . .

Mitch gave a happy little hum and then sighed, shifting slightly to get more comfortable. A few moments later, he began breathing more deeply, and I realized he'd fallen asleep with his cock inside me.

Trapped in Mitch's whiskey-scented embrace, I stared blindly into the dark, feeling like I was losing my mind. I had to be because what else would explain the torrent of conflicting emotions I felt?

I woke up with a gasp and lay there wide-eyed in the dark, wondering what had jolted me out of sleep—a glance at my phone showed we'd only been asleep about an hour.

"Hey!" Mitch suddenly barked out, startling me, and his arm jerked me back hard. "Uh. Mm. Uh, *no*," he mumbled quietly, then exhaled hard.

It took me a second to realize Mitch was sleep-talking, something he'd never done before. I waited a bit, and when he didn't say anything else, I shut my eyes.

"No! Huh *huh*. Huh-*no*."

Damn.

Mitch muttered something unintelligible, stopped, and then made a harsh noise in the back of his throat.

I wondered what he was dreaming about. It didn't sound good.

"No. Nuh-nuh . . . Mmm nuh-*no*. *Please*."

It was only then that I noticed Mitch's dick was still inside me because it started to swell and harden.

I winced. "Ow. Mitch? Mitch, wake up."

"Huh. *No!*" Mitch's body bucked against me, his legs beginning to thrash as his arm tightened around me, his cock stretching me open. "No. *Huh*. Stop. Stop. *Stop!*" he said with a whimper. He was silent for a few seconds, then he started gasping and shaking the bed . . . and abruptly stopped with a jerk.

"Fuck," he whispered, breathing hard for a few moments, apparently awake. Then he groaned and let out a shuddering sigh before grabbing me by the hip to start fucking me, not bothering to check if I was awake or not.

Stunned, I just lay there silently as he thrust four or five times before he let out a soft grunt, cumming quietly inside me. He waited a few seconds, panting slowly, then pulled away and rolled over.

I cleared my throat. "Mitch?"

Mitch started snoring.

Turning onto my back, I frowned at the ceiling, my ass warm and throbbing with my heartbeat. I felt degraded and used . . . *exactly* the feelings I sought out when I offered my ass to strangers in the park, but tenfold.

I grabbed my dick and came almost instantly.

CHAPTER 13
IN THE CLOSET

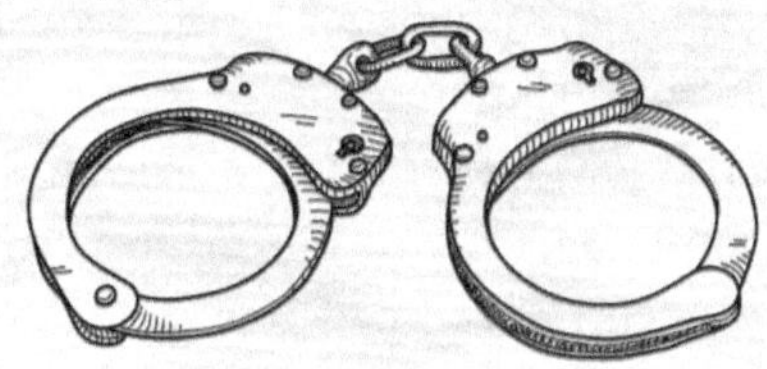

DECEMBER

MITCH and I were waiting by the counter at the Italian butcher shop for our sausage subs when a voice called out.

"Well, I'll be damned! Fuckin' Michel McKenzie!"

We both turned to the man stomping snow off his boots by the door.

"Freddy!" Mitch exclaimed, smiling as the man walked towards us with a wide grin on his fleshy face. The two of them did the shoulder-check bro-hug, complete with a firm slap to each other's backs before letting go. Freddy was as tall as Mitch but wider, especially around the middle, and had the same dark hair and Roman nose. They *had* to be related.

"How ya been?" Freddy asked, unzipping the top of his jacket. It looked like he was wearing a uniform underneath. "Shit, Michel, I haven't seen you in fuckin' *ages* it feels like."

Mitch chuckled. "Yeah, I think it was that May two-four barbecue at Jenny's?"

"Shit yeah. Man, you got *hammered*."

"Me? You're the one who went swimming in his jeans, you fucktard."

They both laughed then Freddy noticed me watching them.

"Hey. Who's your friend?"

Smiling, Mitch turned to me. "Oh, this is Patrick. The SPVM's doing this thing with underprivileged youth, you know? Spending time with them and shit like that."

"No shit?" Freddy's mouth turned down at the corners as he nodded, looking impressed. "Like a Big Brothers thing?"

"Yeah, exactly." Mitch clapped me on the shoulder. "I'm teaching this little shit all about being responsible and, you know, not winding up a smackhead on the street."

I sighed inwardly.

Freddy grinned at me. "You should get Michel here to sneak you into a titty bar," he said with a wink. He pronounced it *tiddy*.

Mitch laughed. "Yeah, maybe I should." He smirked at me, his eyes narrowed in mirth. "Make a man out of you, eh?"

"Here you go! Two sausage subs with extra peppers and a Brio." The woman behind the counter held out a paper bag.

"Oh, thank you," I said, taking the bag from her.

"Well, we gotta jet, man," Mitch said, holding his hand out. "Take care of yourself, Freddy. Say hi to your ma for me."

Freddy shook Mitch's hand. "You bet. Patty, nice to meetcha."

"You too," I said, smiling, then followed Mitch out of the shop. The snow had stopped and the sun had come out—everything was sharp and bright and pretty.

"So who was *that*?" I asked as I got into the passenger seat of Mitch's Corolla.

"Oh . . . that's my cousin Freddy." Mitch dug through the bag, pulled out a sub, and handed it to me.

"Why did he keep calling you 'Michel'?"

Mitch frowned. "Because that's my name," he replied, then took a big bite of his sub. He let out a happy moan as he chewed.

"*Fuck* they make the best fucking subs," he said with his mouth full.

"So, Mitch is just a nickname?"

Mitch swallowed and sighed. "When my mum had me, my dad was out doing the peacekeeper thing in Cyprus because of that coup in seventy-four. So he wasn't around when I was born. Mum named me after some singer she was into, and when my dad found out, he was *pissed*. Thought the name was too faggoty." He took another bite of his sub.

"Can we *not* with the f-word?"

"He thought it was a *sissy* name," Mitch replied. "Better?"

"Not really. But go on."

"So he started calling me Mitch. I don't think he called me Michel once in his life. Everyone just knows me as Mitch."

"And Freddy thinks Michel is effeminate too and calls you that to fuck with you?"

"Yeah. Freddy's a real asshole," Mitch said and wiped the corner of his mouth with his thumb. "His dad and my dad were brothers."

"Were?"

Mitch nodded. "My dad passed uh . . . oh *shit*." He frowned. "He would have been my age now. Heart attack. Freddy's old man kicked it the same way a year later." Mitch rubbed his knuckles against the left side of his chest, his gaze distant for a moment.

"So . . . your dad was a soldier?" I asked.

"Yeah. A soldier first, and then he became a cop after he was honourably discharged. My sister's a cop too. Jenny lives out in Saint-Hyacinthe with her husband Laurent . . . They got two kids. Rémi and uhhh . . ."—Mitch's lips twisted to the side, and he closed his eyes as he thought for a moment—"the other one."

I laughed. "Uncle of the year."

Mitch grinned and shrugged, balling up the sandwich wrapping and dropping it in the bag. He retrieved the Brio and popped the tab, taking a big swig.

"I don't know how you can drink that," I said, making a face. "Tastes like medicine."

Mitch thumped his chest and let out a loud burp. "More for me."

"Is Freddy a cop too?" I asked to keep Mitch talking—it was rare that he shared anything about himself with me and I wanted to know more.

"*Was* a cop." Mitch put his drink into the cup holder and keyed the engine, checking over his shoulder before pulling out into traffic. "He was a dirty cop and he got caught."

"Oh yeah?"

"Yeah, he accepted a bribe or some shit from someone connected to the Rizzutos."

"What . . . like the Mafia?"

"Yes, dumbass. *Exactly* like that. Now he's a fucking mall cop." Mitch glanced over at me with a wide grin. "Hey, you've got sauce on your chin."

"Oh. Thanks." I wiped my face with my napkin, then I wrapped up the other half of my sub.

"What are you doing?"

"I'm saving the rest for later."

"No. You're going to eat it right now," Mitch replied, changing lanes.

"I promise I won't leave it in here." He had been *seriously* annoyed when I'd left half my smoked meat sandwich in his car overnight. Mitch had called it a waste and he *loathed* waste.

"Patrick, you're too fucking skinny. Have you seen yourself? There was more meat back there on the butcher's apron than there is on your bones." He shook his head. "From now on, you're going to finish every meal. And I don't want to hear any fucking complaints."

I stared wide-eyed at his profile. Was he serious?

Mitch felt my eyes on him and shot me a glance. He smirked and reached over to squeeze my thigh.

"Listen . . . I'd like a little more padding when I'm fucking you, okay?"

I swallowed, staring at his hand on my leg, and breathed through the sudden tightness in my chest, wondering if he could tell my dick was getting hard.

"Um. Okay," I replied softly, unwrapping my sausage sub.

"Good boy," he said and patted my thigh before pulling his hand away.

My face felt hot as I took a big bite, forcing myself to eat even though I wasn't hungry, and chewed quickly to distract myself from the thought of Mitch's cock inside me.

"And . . ." I swallowed. "Uh. What about your mom?"

"What about her?"

"Is she still around?"

Mitch nodded. "She lives in fucking Florida with her new husband Carlos." From the way he said it, it was clear he didn't approve.

"Oh." I sat there in awkward silence for a few seconds, wondering how I could get the conversation going again. "Um, my parents live in the West Island. My dad's a chartered accountant, and my mom works in a flower shop. And um, I have two sisters . . . I'm the middle child."

Mitch snorted. "Of course you are."

I frowned at him. "Why 'of course'?"

"Middle kids are needy people pleasers."

"What? Who says that?"

"Everyone." Mitch turned on his blinkers and merged onto the highway. After a moment, he turned on the radio.

Shit. I'd changed the station the other day when he'd made me wait while he picked up some stuff from a storage unit he had rented, and I must have just turned it off instead of switching it back to CHOM.

"Fuck. I'm sorry," I said, reaching for the knob.

"It's okay," he replied, checking his blind spot before getting into the fast lane. "I like Depeche Mode."

"You do?" I sat back in my seat and smiled. "Cool. I like Depeche Mode too."

I was surprised when the song finished and he didn't change the station.

Huh. "So hey, uh, should I start calling you Michel?" I asked teasingly.

Mitch smirked. "Go ahead. See what happens."

I chuckled and then quickly craned my neck to the right, wondering if I had read the sign right.

"Are we going to Laval?" I asked.

Mitch nodded.

"Why? Where are we going?"

"You'll see."

I stared up at the house. It was a massive grey-stone building with a dark red peaked roof and arched windows. From the way the falling snow melted immediately on contact with the walkway and two-car driveway, I guessed they were heated.

"Jesus," I said quietly. "Cops make more money than I thought." I grinned, looking over at Mitch. "Or are you getting a little somethin' on the side from the Rizzutos too?"

"That's not funny, Patrick." Mitch gave me a stony glare. "I'm not a dirty cop."

I blinked at him, thinking about the day we met, but I kept my mouth shut.

Something about the realtor on the For Sale sign reminded me of the "women laughing with salads" meme that had gone around a few years back. The woman—whose name was Nour Khemiri, according to the sign—was pretty, with long dark hair and olive skin, but her red-lipsticked smile looked a little maniacal because it didn't reach her eyes.

"So . . ." I stuck my hands in my coat pockets, looking up at the house again. "What are we doing here?"

"My ex-wife is selling the place, so she wants me to clear out the rest of my shit."

"Oh." I followed Mitch up the walkway and stepped inside once he'd unlocked the door. We left our boots and coats in the foyer and headed to the kitchen first. Mitch opened the massive steel fridge and stared at the food on the shelves.

"You left something in there?"

"Nope." Mitch slammed the fridge shut, then grabbed an apple from the bowl on the kitchen island. He took a big bite and put it back.

I laughed. "Petty."

Mitch just shrugged. "Come on. Let's go upstairs."

He led me up the wide, curving staircase, and I paused near the top to look at a framed picture. The woman from the For Sale sign was sitting on a wrought iron bench in front of a fountain. Her hair was in a thick braid over her shoulder, and her feet were bare. The smile she wore in this photo was *way* more genuine than the one in her headshot on the sign.

"Your ex-wife is the real estate agent?" I asked, looking up. Mitch was nowhere to be seen. "Hello?" I said, looking into the first room, but it was empty except for some workout equipment. "Mitch?" The next room was a very large bathroom with two sinks and a jacuzzi tub.

The third door led to the master bedroom, featuring a king-size bed on a raised platform.

"Hello?"

"I'm in the closet," came Mitch's reply.

I let out a laugh. "No kidding."

"What was that?" Mitch asked, stepping out of the walk-in closet carrying a big Rubbermaid tub.

"Nothing," I said with a smile. "So, your ex is the one actually selling the house? I saw her picture."

"Yeah. She's one of the top agents in Laval." Mitch returned to the closet and came back with some ties and a pair of dress shoes. "Which means she'll get a good price for this place. Unless, of course, she chooses to lowball it just to fuck me over."

"Oh, you're getting some money from the sale?"

"Half, yeah."

"How much do you think it'll sell for?" I looked around the bedroom. It was as big as my whole apartment.

"A million-five. Maybe more," Mitch said, throwing some dress shirts into the storage bin.

"Holy shit." I grinned. "What are you going to do with your riches?"

Mitch paused in his packing, contemplating, then he shrugged. "I dunno. I'm not much of a materialist."

"Yeah, I know," I said, eyeing the expensive-looking furniture and gold-curlicued accents on the drapes and bedding. "Which is why I just *cannot* imagine you living here."

"Oh . . . that's all Nour. Trust me." He opened a hinged box on the bed and shuffled through the papers inside. A photograph fell out and I picked it up. A young, slim Mitch smiled at the camera with his arm slung over the shoulders of a young woman who was holding her hand over the bottom of her face, apparently laughing. Her dark hair was loose and fanned out to the side like it was very windy.

"This her too?" I held out the photo.

Mitch took it from me, staring down at the happy couple with a sigh. "Yep."

"How long were you together?"

"Since high school. And uh . . . married thirty years. Well, *would* have been thirty years this January." Mitch placed the photo face down in the box and pulled out a few envelopes. Then he put the box back in the closet.

"You married your high school sweetheart? Wow."

"I did." Mitch rummaged through one of the nightstands and came back with a watch and some headphones.

"I'm sorry. You probably don't want to talk about it."

"It's fine." Mitch put his things in the bin before going to the long dresser across the room to go through the drawers there.

"No kids?"

"I would have been a shit dad," Mitch replied, shooting a glance over his shoulder at me.

I shrugged. "Who knows."

"Nour wanted kids but I put my foot down. I think that was the beginning of the end, even though it took us a few decades to realize it."

"Yeah?" I watched him rifle through the dresser.

"She always did her thing, and I did my thing and stayed out of her way . . . and then all of a sudden, it's thirty years later, and I can't remember the last time I've had a conversation with my wife." Mitch dropped some socks into the bin and closed the lid.

"I'm sorry."

"Don't be," he replied with a smile. "I don't care." Mitch tilted his head and narrowed his eyes at me.

"What?"

"Maybe we could take a vacation."

"Sorry?" I raised my eyebrows.

"You know . . . with some of my 'riches'."

"*Ohh.*" I stepped towards him. "You mean me and you?"

Mitch nodded and I threw my arms around his neck, looking up at him with a coy grin.

"Where would we go?" I asked, running my fingers gently through the hair at his nape.

Mitch's pupils dilated as he gazed down at me. "Uhh. I was thinking . . . maybe Greece?"

"Greece?"

"Yeah. So that we could uh . . . you know . . ."—his face flushed—"be out in public?"

I blinked at him for a second, thinking he meant sex, but then it dawned on me what he was talking about.

"So that we can be 'gay' in public. Is that what you mean?" I said teasingly.

He cleared his throat. "Well. Not *gay*. Just . . ." Mitch huffed out his breath, visibly flummoxed.

I hopped up and wrapped my legs around Mitch's waist, and he caught me, supporting my backside with his hands. I chuckled and pecked a kiss next to his lips.

"Mitch, we can be out in public *here*, you know. It's Montreal, not like . . . Alabama or whatever. Or Somalia. No one's going to give a *shit* if they see us kiss. I mean, besides . . . have you *seen* yourself? It's not like you're a small guy. I'm pretty sure you'd send any homophobe running with one of your big, mean cop scowls if they were stupid enough to say anything."

Mitch's brow furrowed. "It's not that."

"Oh. Then, you're worried that people you know will find out that you spend your free time deep-dicking a twink with your massive cock?"

"Jesus." Mitch barked a laugh but then immediately sobered. "I just want to keep things . . . private."

"Those cops you brought to the motel know you fuck me," I pointed out.

"I've got so much shit on them that they'd be screwed six ways from Sunday if they said anything." Mitch frowned. "And don't ever bring that up again, Patrick. I mean it."

"*Fine*. Okay. We'll go to Greece." I smiled. "But . . . why do older guys suggest *Greece*? Is it an old gay Mecca or something? Why not like, Provincetown . . . or, um, Fire Island? Why is it always *Greece*?"

"Wait—what other guy is suggesting Greece to you?" Mitch replied, his smile fading.

"Hey, you don't know what I get up to when you're not around . . ."

Mitch's eyes widened.

"I'm kidding. I'm kidding," I said quickly. "I'm totally kidding,"

He studied my expression. "You better be."

"I wouldn't dare."

"Good." He said with a nod. Then his gaze lowered, focusing on my lips, and I knew what he wanted from me.

I leaned in for a kiss, and Mitch let out a low growl, attacking my tongue with his and forcing my head back in his eagerness. I moaned, raking his back and he squeezed my ass hard in response. Turning around, he walked us to the bed and climbed onto it with me clinging to him from below like a baby monkey.

Mitch then collapsed on top of me and began smothering me with kisses, nuzzling into the sides of my neck and behind my ears until I was giggling and struggling to get free. Finally, he pulled back, his eyes dark with lust, and pushed his hard bulge against my ass.

"My 'massive' cock wants your 'twink' ass," he said softly, nudging me with his dick.

"Does it now?" I replied, then gasped as he leaned in to bite the side of my neck none too gently. "Ow!"

Chuckling against my throat, Mitch nodded. "It does."

"You want to fuck on your ex-wife's bed?" I said, yelping as he bit me again. "*Ow* fuck."

"I don't care," he replied, getting up on his knees. "Take your pants off."

"Hang on," I said, an idea forming. "Why don't you lie down there." I pointed. "On your back."

"Oh?" Mitch's brows rose slowly.

I pulled myself backwards and swung my legs off the side of the bed, standing so I could get undressed.

Mitch stared at me for a moment, looking unconvinced.

"Go on. On your back."

Grumbling to himself, Mitch took off his shirt and stretched out on his back, lacing his fingers behind his head to watch me strip down to my skin. Then, smiling in a way that I hoped was seductive, I crawled up onto the mattress to straddle his thighs. I undid his belt and button, then slowly unzipped his fly, loving the way his lips parted slightly as his eyes tracked my hands. I moved back a bit so I could lean down and kiss his furry belly above the waistband of his boxers, then further down, skimming my lips over his thick, cloth-covered erection.

"*F-fuck.*" The word hitched in Mitch's throat as I pushed my mouth harder against his dick, blowing a hot breath through the fabric. "Patrick?"

"Yes?" I asked, looking up.

"I don't like being teased."

I stared at him for a beat. "Okay. Sorry. I was just . . . trying something."

"Well, try faster."

I let out a snort and shook my head. "*So* fucking impatient." I traced the head of his dick slowly through his boxers with my finger.

"I swear to Christ . . . Do you *want* me to hold you down and make you cry?" Mitch asked in a quiet voice, the promise of violence clear in his pale blue gaze.

Rolling my eyes to cover my nervousness, I dragged his jeans down to midthigh, then did the same with his boxers. His dick bobbed up from his belly a few times as I moved closer, and I wrapped my hand around it to begin stroking him quickly and firmly.

"This better?" I asked.

"I'd rather be rearranging your insides."

However, from the way precum ran down his shaft as I squeezed him, I gathered he was enjoying himself more than he let on. "So . . . where can a guy find some lube around here?"

Mitch frowned, thinking. "Try under the bed."

I got off Mitch and ducked down to look under the bed and found a big zippered case. I pulled it towards me and opened it, grimacing when I encountered a pile of candy-coloured sex toys. I jiggled the case a bit so I didn't have to touch anything and found a small bottle of lube resting between a clear pink vibrator filled with white pearls and a bright purple butt plug. Using two fingers, I extricated the bottle and climbed back on top of Mitch. I took his dick out of his hands and covered it well with lube, then I inched forward until the head was pointed up at my hole. I slowly eased myself down until his dick was resting against my pucker and then stayed put, just gently moving my pelvis back and forth . . . teasing.

I knew I was asking for it.

Sure enough, Mitch let out a growl of frustration and grabbed me by the hips, forcing me down so hard that his cock punched straight up into my guts, all the way to the root.

I gasped then cried out, my thighs trembling as my hole spasmed painfully around Mitch's dick. Clenching my jaw, I leaned forward, tears blurring my vision, straining to breathe through the abrupt penetration.

"Well?" Mitch growled after a moment. "Are you just going to sit there, or what?"

I shook my head, rising up on my knees to start riding Mitch's cock like my life depended on it. He began eagerly pushing up into me hard when I came down, his soft moans spurring me on, making me wonder why I'd never tried this with him before. Soon, my boner was bouncing up and down, slapping against Mitch's stomach and flinging little drops of precum onto his chest as I moved.

My hole began feeling all loose and warm, and every time I reached the base of Mitch's shaft, the stretch felt *so* good. Sweat poured down between my shoulder blades, and my hair stuck to my forehead as I forced myself to move faster, my breath coming in loud gasps as my pleasure started to build. My thighs were burning, but I ignored the pain as I used Mitch's thick cock to drive myself to orgasm.

So close.

I let out a groan, impaling myself hard as my balls tightened and my dick swelled.

"Oh my god . . . *huhh* ohmygod," I said, gasping as all my pelvic muscles contracted at once, then wailed as the hot liquid pulse erupted from my core, sending a shockwave into my ass. My hole gripped Mitch's shaft and I cried out as I began spurting cum all over his belly, the throbbing climax so immense that I was shaking hard by the end of it.

Mitch's mouth opened as he stared at the mess I'd made all over him, his brow furrowed, and for one breathless second I thought he was pissed off, but then he threw his head back and grunted through clenched teeth, his eyes tightly shut as his dick twitched inside me, breeding me deep as I sat there panting and shivering.

In that instant, he was the most gorgeous thing in the world, and all his transgressions were forgiven—at least temporarily—as I watched him moan through his orgasm.

He came from watching me cum. I was pretty proud of myself.

Mitch blew out a slow breath, coming back to earth as his body relaxed beneath me. He opened his eyes, looking a little dazed, then chuckled softly.

"Oof." He suddenly spasmed, then trembled, wincing. "Okay . . . get off."

I quickly climbed off him and he tugged gently on his softening dick, grimacing as he covered the head with his foreskin. Then he frowned, staring down at his cum-covered stomach. Sighing, he stood and dug under one of the pillows until he pulled out something made from satiny peach fabric.

I raised my brows in amusement as he mopped the cum from his belly with what was apparently his ex-wife's nightie.

"I was sure you were going to make me clean you off with my tongue."

Mitch paused and lifted his head. "Why? Do you *want* to?"

I laughed. "No. No, thank you." Then I frowned. "Won't she be pissed off when she sees that? What if we get in trouble? What if *I* get in trouble?"

"Why?" Mitch balled up the nightie and dumped it in the hamper.

"That's my DNA on there," I replied with a nervous laugh

Mitch snorted. "This isn't a crime scene, dipshit." He grabbed his jeans from the bed. "Besides . . . why would anyone have your DNA? What the fuck would you have done to get in the system? Commit a bunch of crimes lately?"

"Oh." I chuckled. "Yeah, no." I stood to get the clothes I'd left on the floor.

Mitch surprised me when he reached out to cup the back of my neck in his big, warm hand. His eyes narrowed as he looked down at me.

"So . . . that was good."

"Yeah?" I beamed up at him.

"Yeah." He pulled me towards him to press a kiss to my temple. "Now, let's get the fuck outta Dodge, eh? I got what I wanted. The bitch can burn the rest for all I care."

Thankfully, the traffic wasn't bad crossing the bridge from Laval back to Montreal, and we made good time getting back to NDG. However, we were still ten minutes from the apartment when we stopped at a red light, and things started getting . . . *weird* with Mitch.

Two guys were standing on the corner of the street, talking and holding hands. I noticed Mitch's eyes narrowing as he watched them, his hands gripping the steering wheel hard. Then one of the guys laughed and leaned in to kiss the other guy, and the muscles bunched in Mitch's jaw.

Uh oh. I wondered whether it was a good idea to point out that the guys kissing just proved my point about Montreal earlier, but then the car behind us honked, and Mitch swore and stomped on the gas. He sent the Corolla fishtailing across the intersection, causing the two guys to leap back from the edge of the sidewalk in alarm.

Staring stonily ahead, Mitch swerved around a big pickup truck and nearly clipped the bumper of a Kia in the next lane.

"Fucker," he growled and tapped the horn with the side of his fist as he passed the Kia. Then he glared at the radio as "Dance The Night" by Dua Lipa came on. He growled and hit the AUX button, then fumbled his phone out of his pocket as he veered suddenly left to avoid a pothole.

I clung to the door handle and my seatbelt chest strap as the Corolla sped along doing at least twice the speed limit.

"Mitch? Uh . . . what's the matter?" I asked, my voice high with fright. I wanted to close my eyes but I couldn't.

"Didn't want to listen to your *shitty* music," he replied, his anger palpable. He stuck his phone in the cheap plastic holder as his music began to play, and thumbed the volume up while barely touching the brake at the next stop sign.

"Oh my god," I said, wincing as I was jostled when we hit a speed bump hard.

Finally, we screeched to a halt in front of the apartment, but Mitch didn't kill the engine. He just sat there glaring through the windshield. On the stereo, the singer was screaming, "Don't you tell me how I feel" over and over again.

"What are we doing?" I asked nervously.

"*We* are not doing anything," Mitch said tersely. "*You're* getting out of my fucking car."

"Oh." I frowned, undoing my seatbelt. Then I swallowed, licking my lips before asking, "Where are you going?"

"I'm going to the gym."

CHAPTER 14
A REAL MAN

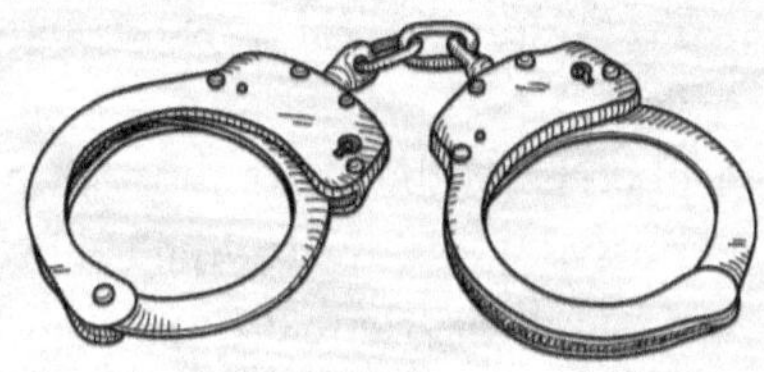

I WOKE up to voices in the apartment and turned over, blearily squinting at the time on my phone. It was just past three in the morning. I lifted my head and listened—I recognized Mitch's voice but couldn't hear the person he was talking to.

What the fuck?

Still half asleep, I dragged myself out of bed, pulled a pair of joggers on over my boxers and grabbed a T-shirt. Yanking the latter down over my head, I trudged out to the living room to see what the hell was going on and stopped in my tracks. Mitch was sitting on the couch with a woman straddling him. I frowned—her skirt was hiked up to her hips, and her red thong was on the couch next to Mitch.

"Mitch?" I said, my voice rough with sleep.

The woman gasped and twisted around as Mitch looked over her shoulder with a big shit-eating grin.

"Heyyy Patrick," he said, chuckling. He was plainly drunk. "What's up, dipshit?"

"So 'going to the gym' is just code for 'getting shitfaced,' now, eh?" I said, crossing my arms. I clenched my jaw, meeting the gaze of the woman. She was probably around Mitch's age and fairly pretty with long, strawberry blond hair, big dark eyes, and a pouty bottom lip.

"Oh, fuck *off*," Mitch slurred, squeezing the woman's backside with both hands. "M'busy getting some pussy."

The woman turned back to him with a laugh. "Not yet, you're not. Not without a condom, I said." She spoke with a faint Québécois French accent.

Mitch blew a raspberry. "Ugh, I hate those things."

"No condom, no pussy," she said, wiggling her behind. She glanced back at me again. "And your little friend has to go. He looks underage."

I sighed. "Why does everyone think I'm so young?"

"He's plenty old enough," Mitch said, then he hiccupped. "Aren't you, Patrick? Maybe it's time to learn about the birds and the bees, eh? Have you never even seen a pussy 'fore that wasn't yer mommy's?" he said, grinning at me.

Curling my lip at him, I turned to go. "Fuck this," I muttered.

"No!"

I looked back at Mitch and saw that he'd pushed the woman off his lap. After a few failed attempts, he got to his feet and stood in the centre of the living room, his face contorted in fury as he pointed a wavering finger at me.

"No. You fucking come *here*, Patrick. You're going to sit in this chair," he said, grabbing the back of one of the dining chairs and dragging it unsteadily toward the couch. "You're going to sit in this chair . . . Yeah, sit in this *cuck* chair and watch me fuck her." He jabbed a finger in her direction. "That's what you're going to do. I'm gonna show you how a real man fucks." It seemed like the only things keeping him upright were his anger and the chair he was clinging to. "Show you a real man fucks *pussy*."

Meanwhile, the woman was watching the exchange with clear worry on her face. She reached for her underwear and slid them towards her. The motion caught Mitch's attention, and his expression changed from anger to apologetic in an instant.

"No. It's okay. It's okay. He's my *roommate*," he said, flapping a hand in my direction. "He'll sit quiet and watch. I promise. It's good for him. And"—he pulled his wallet from his back pocket—"I'll pay you extra for him to watch. And maybe"—he hiccupped again and laughed, swaying—"he can fuck you too."

The woman shook her head slowly. "I'm sorry, no. That's not going to happen."

"Aww, c'mon, sweetheart. Look . . . *look*," Mitch picked up a wrapped condom from the coffee table and tore it open. "Look, I'll be good and wear one. Watch."

The woman and I silently watched Mitch drop his pants and attempt to roll a condom over his limp dick. We shared a look—no doubt my expression mirrored the misgiving in hers.

"Shit," Mitch muttered to himself, turning the condom over like that was the problem and not his lack of erection. "Fuck." He dropped the half-unrolled condom on the floor and stooped to pick it up, but ended up landing on his side on the couch instead. Smiling, he grabbed the woman's arm. "Hey honey, wanna give me a little head to warm up? C'mon," he said, tugging her arm playfully.

The woman shot me a look. She seemed more uneasy than afraid, but she clearly wanted me to step in.

"Mitch, it's late," I said. "Let uh . . ." I met the woman's eyes, prompting her for a name. It felt like I was negotiating a hostage situation: *humanize the hostage.*

"Mélanie," she said quietly.

"Let Mélanie go home. Maybe you and me can see her another day, and then yeah, maybe you can show me what I've been missing all these years, eh? C'mon, Mitch. Let her go." I reached for Mitch's hand. He'd closed his eyes and, for a second, I thought he'd passed out.

Mitch let out a long whiskey-scented sigh and shook his head slowly, pushing me away and dropping the woman's arm. It was like all the anger had suddenly gone out of him, and he just lay there, limp and quiet.

Mélanie stood, quickly pulling on her panties before stuffing the rest of the condoms and a pack of cigarettes into her little red purse.

"I'm going to bed," Mitch muttered. He got off the couch and weaved his way to the bedroom without another word, slamming the door behind him.

I let out a sigh of relief and turned to the woman.

"I am so sorry about him," I said, walking her to the front door. "He's got issues."

"You're telling *me*," Mélanie replied, twisting her lips to the side. "Thanks for the assist." She bent over to pull on her tall boots, using my arm to steady herself.

"It's no problem. Really." I stood there awkwardly, scratching the back of my head. "I uh . . . don't mean to assume, but um, he mentioned money earlier. Does that mean . . ."

"That I'm a sex worker?" Mélanie smiled. "I am. Is that a problem?"

"No!" I blurted out quickly. "No. Not at all. I just wanted to make sure you got paid and everything."

"I did. I always ask for money up front."

"Okay, good." I watched her put her winter coat on. "Can I get you an Uber or something?"

"Sure. I would love that."

I found Mitch's phone in his pants on the floor and keyed in his password to order a car for Mélanie.

"It'll be here in eight minutes," I said, showing her the screen. "A blue Subaru. You can wait in here until it comes. You know . . . stay warm." I smiled.

"That's okay," the woman replied. "I'll go have a smoke while I'll wait. Thanks again. And uh, *bonne chance* with Mitch." She squeezed my arm, looking into my eyes. "He's your boyfriend?"

I shrugged. "I don't know what he is."

"Be careful," Mélanie said, smiling softly in sympathy.

I didn't know what else to do but nod.

"Oh, and we're *not* meeting up again, us three," she added, arching an eyebrow at me. "Not ever."

Chuckling, I nodded again. "No, I know that. I just said that to make him stop."

"Okay. *Bon* . . . take care of yourself."

As she stepped out the door, I asked, "Hey, what would you have done if I wasn't there?"

She stopped and looked back at me, pulling her pack of Du Mauriers out of her purse. She deftly slipped a cigarette out and tucked it between her lips, lighting it with a small pink lighter.

"I can take care of myself," she said with a coy narrowing of her eyes. "Don't you worry about me. But, I always prefer a peaceful end to things and not have to pull out the pepper spray." She tilted her open purse to show me the little canister within.

I blinked. It wasn't pepper spray—it was *bear* spray.

Mélanie just winked and took another drag of her cigarette, then went down the front steps, leaving me to deal with the drunken asshole in my bedroom.

Our bedroom. I sighed, shutting and locking the front door.

I threw the crumb-and-dust-covered condom in the garbage, then turned off the lights. I squared my shoulders and stared at the bedroom door for a moment, steeling myself. I *really* hoped he was asleep.

After quietly opening the door, I stepped inside the darkened room and promptly stumbled over Mitch lying curled up on his side on the bare floor.

"Shit." I leaned over and put a hand on his shoulder, assuming he'd passed out on the floor and that, hopefully, a good shake would wake him, but my heart stopped when I felt him shuddering. Thinking Mitch was having a seizure or something, I clicked on the light and dropped to my knees next to him. I turned him over then sat back on my heels, staring down at Mitch's tear-streaked face.

Mitch let out a quavering breath, blinking up at me, his eyes swollen from crying.

"I don't want to be gay," he whispered and then burst into fresh tears.

I could only stare at first, not believing my eyes, then I quickly slid him closer, hefting his head and shoulders into my lap so I could hold him while he wept brokenly in my arms.

CHAPTER 15
A COUPLE OF LOSERS

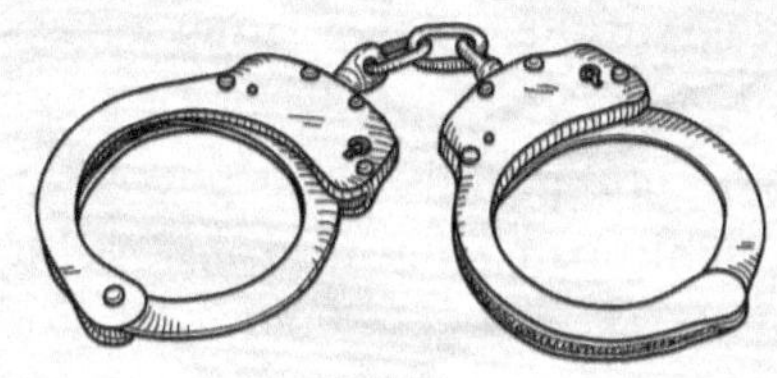

When I woke up the next morning, Mitch was still asleep next to me. I stared at the back of his head, listening to his breathing. I'd managed to coax him into bed when his tears had tapered off, and he'd passed out almost immediately, leaving me to lie there in a daze for a long time.

I sighed. I *still* didn't know how to feel about everything that had happened. Did I feel sympathy for Mitch? Yes. Was I pissed off at him? Also, yes. And, knowing Mitch, he wouldn't want to talk about any of it, which made the whole thing even more frustrating.

Shaking my head, I inched forward until I was close to Mitch and gently put my arm around his waist.

However, as soon as I had settled against him, he let out a quiet grunt and pulled away from me. He got out of bed and, without a backwards glance, left the room.

I shut my eyes.

I must have fallen asleep waiting for Mitch because when I opened my eyes again, it was almost forty minutes later. Mitch hadn't come back to bed. He hadn't left, though—I could hear the TV faintly playing.

I got up and got dressed, feeling nervous because I had no idea what to expect from Mitch in the aftermath of . . . whatever that was last night.

Mitch was sitting on the couch wearing a McGill University T-shirt and a pair of grey sweatpants I'd never seen before. His hair stuck up on one side, and the salt and pepper in his beard made his overlong stubble look patchy against his sickly pale skin—he looked pretty rough. An episode of *Hoarders* was playing on the television.

"Hi."

Mitch glanced at me and gave me a curt nod in greeting, then went back to his show.

I frowned and folded my arms, rubbing my biceps anxiously. "So . . . um . . . *listen*, about last ni—"

"I don't want to talk about it."

"Of course, you don't," I muttered. Sighing, I stepped closer. "You were being really shitty to that woman."

"I said I didn't want to talk about it," he growled without looking at me.

"You're lucky she didn't spray you."

Mitch blinked a few times, then turned to me with a scowl. "*What* did you say?"

"Um . . . that you were lucky she didn't spray you?" I gave a nervous laugh.

"Did she *say* she had pepper spray on her?"

Well, bear spray, but . . . "Uh, she had some, yeah."

"It's *illegal.*"

"Oh. I didn't know that."

"It's a prohibited weapon. You can go to jail if you're caught with it."

Oh shit. I stared at him for a few seconds, feeling like a complete idiot. *Did I just fuck Mélanie over?*

"Mitch, please tell me you're not going to go hunt her down for having pepper spray. You were being really awful to her last night—just . . . can you just leave her be, please?"

Turning his focus back to the people on TV crawling over a nearly ceiling-high pile of clothing, he lifted one shoulder in a tiny shrug. "Don't give a shit."

It wasn't clear whether he meant he didn't care about the spray or my request, but I decided not to push it.

"How're you feeling?" I asked.

"I'm fine."

"Okay." I stood there awkwardly for a moment. "Have you eaten? Do you want something?"

"No."

"All right." I went into the kitchen and pulled out my knockoff Froot Loops, but before I could pour myself a bowl, Mitch interrupted me.

"Patrick, you're not eating that."

I turned around, my eyes wide—he was watching me from the couch.

"Um. I'm not?"

"That shit'll kill you. From now on, you're going to eat better," he replied, turning his attention back to the show.

"I thought you wanted me to fatten up? Isn't junk food fattening?" I studied the nutrition label, then made a face. *Ew.*

"Not with your metabolism," Mitch said. "You need to eat *well* to gain weight."

"Is that so? You're a nutrition expert now?"

Mitch didn't reply.

I opened the fridge and looked dubiously at the very old carton of eggs on the top shelf.

"So . . . what am I supposed to eat?"

"Figure it out."

Scowling, I went back to the living room. "Fine. I'll go to the store." I held out my hand.

"What?"

"Can I have some money, please?"

"Take my card," Mitch said, jerking his chin toward his wallet on the coffee table. "That reminds me—I'll get you one of your own."

"What? A bank card? I have one." Not that I had a cent to my name, though.

"A card for *my* account. That way, I can monitor your spending."

"Monitor . . . my spending?" I stared at him. "Are you for real?"

His flinty expression answered for him.

"If I have to rely on you for money, why don't you just give me an allowance or something?" I asked.

"Because you're not a fucking child, Patrick."

"And you want to 'monitor' my spending?" Annoyed, I yanked his bank card out and tossed his wallet back on the coffee table. "Do you even *hear* yourself?"

"What was that?" Mitch turned his cold gaze on me.

"I said I'll be right back." *Fuckhead.*

The snow was gone again in typical December fashion—at this rate, Montreal would get another green Christmas. I put up my hood and hurried to the grocery store, dodging around the city workers on the sidewalk as they put up decorations in the rain.

When I got to the store, I quickly grabbed a carton of eggs that was on sale, some bacon, and a loaf of white bread. Staring at the bread for a moment, I decided to get whole wheat instead because that's what Mitch would want me to get. Pleased with myself, I squared my shoulders and started off again but then stopped in my tracks and looked down at the bread in my shopping basket.

Why did following Mitch's stupid rules make me walk a little taller? I gnawed gently on my bottom lip as I stood there, pondering the proud, fluttery feeling I got in my chest every time I did something Mitch approved of. But *why?* Was I just a people pleaser, like he'd said? No . . . pleasing Mitch just hit differently.

Maybe, just maybe, *obeying Mitch makes you happy . . . dumbass.*

I laughed at myself, sighed, and continued down the aisle, picking up some saltines and ginger ale on the way to the cash.

"Pat!" Maude exclaimed as I walked up. "Oh my god, hi."

"Hey." I smiled. "Nice antlers."

She adjusted the sparkly reindeer antlers on her head, batting her eyes at me. "Thanks. They're cute, eh?"

I nodded, unloading my basket onto the rolling counter.

"You never come around anymore," Maude said, pouting. "It's like you totally ghosted us."

"Sorry," I replied, giving her a grimace of apology. "I guess I've been busy?"

"Well, you know it's a good thing you quit when you did . . . Mr. Hoang was going to fire one of us anyway to put in that stupid thing"—she pointed to the new self-checkout cash that had replaced one of the counters—"and it was probably going to be me, so thank you."

I snorted. "Uh, you're welcome? I guess?"

Maude grinned, scanning my items quickly. She saw the name on the bank card I tapped on the Interac machine, and her forehead wrinkled up.

"Using Daddy's card, are we?" Her cheeks dimpled further. "How're things going with your hot cop daddy, anyway?"

I winced faintly at her use of the term and shrugged.

"It's going better?" I said, then thought about the night before. "Or worse? I don't know."

"Sounds complicated."

"You could say that." I bagged up my groceries. "And now he's dictating what I can and can't eat and"—I laughed, shaking my head—"*monitoring my spending,*" I said, using air quotes.

Maude gaped at me, so stunned that she actually stopped chewing her gum for several seconds.

"*What?* Seriously?"

"Yeah," I replied, wondering why telling her about Mitch's rules felt like such a flex. *Huh.* "It's fine."

"*Is* it?" Her voice hit a high note of incredulity.

My gaze lost focus as I stood there, contemplating. How could I put into words what Mitch's increasing control over my life was doing to me? I thought about my decision to buy brown bread instead of white, simply because I thought Mitch would approve.

"Yeah. It is." I smiled at Maude. "It's hard to explain . . . It's like it makes me feel calm and excited."

"How can you be calm *and* excited at the same time?" Maude asked, wrinkling her nose.

"I don't know." I shrugged. "Like I said, it's hard to explain."

"Welp," she said and snapped her gum. "Whatever gets you off, I guess."

I laughed. "Yeah. I guess." I picked up my bag. "Say hi to Khadim for me."

"Will do." Maude crossed her arms and leaned back against the divider, her mouth twisted in a sideways grin as the little gold bells on her antlers jingled. "And don't be a stranger."

I set down the plate and glass on the coffee table in front of Mitch.

Glancing away from his trashy TV, he frowned at my offerings.

"What's that?"

"Saltines and ginger ale," I replied. *Dumbass,* I added mentally and smiled. "To help with your hangover."

"I'm not hungover."

"Uh-huh. Sure," I said, tilting my head at him. "Then why are you squinting like that."

Mitch widened his eyes. "I'm not squinting."

Sighing, I shook my head. "Did you take an Advil?"

"Don't need one."

"It'll make you feel better."

"I feel fine."

I stared at Mitch for a few long seconds. "It won't make you less of a man to take a pill, you know."

Mitch scowled at me. "I don't need one."

Exasperated by his stubbornness, I returned to the kitchen to finish scrambling my eggs. When they were done, I piled them on top of a piece of buttered toast so I wouldn't dirty any more cutlery and went back to the living room. I perched on the arm of the couch with my feet on the cushion while I ate, studying Mitch's profile. He nibbled on the corner of a cracker, made a face, and placed it back on the plate.

When a commercial came on, he muted it and turned to face me.

"*What?*"

I ate the last bite of my egg-on-toast and set my plate down on the couch cushion. "I think you should see a therapist," I said quietly.

"I think you need to keep your fucking opinions to yourself," Mitch snapped back.

"I'm serious. I think it would help you to deal with your . . . trauma"—Mitch snorted at the word—"and all this internalized homophobia. Or . . . *externalized?* Whatever. All-around homophobia. And work through your self-hatred."

Mitch looked at me like I had grown a second head. "The *fuck* are you talking about? Self-hatred? I don't fucking hate myself."

"Really? Because it really feels—"

"*You're* the one who hates himself."

It was my turn to gape at him. "Why do you think I hate myself?"

"Why else would you go to that park and let all those pedos and creeps and perverts stick their dicks in you? I don't know, but that doesn't exactly scream self-respect to me. And to do it over and fucking over again. Jesus, Patrick, how is that *not* self-loathing?"

I narrowed my eyes at him. "Do you not know what a kink is? Or do you rea— *Wait a sec.* How do you know for *sure* I did it more than once?" I had gone cruising a *lot*, sometimes three a week when the weather was nice, but how could he know that? I had lied to him when he caught me, and he hadn't believed me, sure, but there was *something* in his tone just then that made alarm bells go off in my head.

"That night . . . I told you I'd never done it before," I said slowly.

Mitch's lips pressed into a tight line as he glared at me for a moment, his nostrils flaring briefly before he finally replied. "Well, I know for a fact you had."

"Does that mean you saw me before?"

"It's not like you were being super discreet."

"Oh my *god*—you watched me getting fucked before?" My heart was pounding so hard it was making me dizzy.

Mitch didn't answer, but his expression spoke volumes.

"How many times?" I whispered.

"I don't know. I don't remember," he said, sounding defensive. "It's not like I was counting."

"But . . . *how*? I would have noticed a cop. Were you out of uniform?"

After a beat, Mitch nodded reluctantly. "Sometimes. And sometimes I just kept out of sight."

My mind reeled. "Oh my god." I looked down at my balled fists, breathing hard. That meant Mitch sought me out when he was off-duty. I cleared my throat, lifting my eyes to meet his. Obviously, he hadn't fucked me all those times he'd apparently been present—I would have remembered his dick. "So . . . you just got off on stalking me and watching me getting fucked? Is that it?"

Mitch frowned at me, his jaw flexing, not replying.

"And then one day you just . . . *what*?" I said hoarsely, then swallowed hard. "You realized it wasn't getting you off just to watch me anymore? That . . . it was time to *rape* me?"

He scoffed. "I didn't *rape* you, Patrick."

I couldn't believe my ears. "You *blackmailed* me and *forced* me to have sex with you. How is that *not* rape?" I asked, my voice shrill.

Looking bemused, Mitch just stared at me for a moment. A deep wrinkle formed between his dark brows. "You deserved better than those perverts."

"What?" I barked out a harsh laugh. "So you thought I *deserved* being raped by *you* instead?"

"I didn't *rape* you. Stop saying that."

"Mitch, I even *said* it was rape that night. Did you think I was *joking*?"

"I . . ." Doubt was starting to creep into Mitch's expression.

"Do you actually think I *enjoyed* it at all?"

"You enjoy it now," Mitch said in a quiet voice.

"That is a whole other different fucking thing," I replied, wiping away furious tears as I glared at him. "We're not talking about *now*. We're talking about you perving on me all summer in secret. *Fuck.* And *why* were you in the park to begin with?" I didn't know why it hadn't occurred to me before. The more I thought about it, the less it made sense. "You're a Côte Saint-Luc cop, Mitch. Angrignon Park is waaaaay out of your"—I searched for the right word—"*jurisdiction*, no?"

"Actually, it *was* my beat," Mitch replied tersely. "I used to work out of the Ville-Émard station. I patrolled around the park on the regular."

"So, hang on—I don't understand. When did you switch to Côte Saint-Luc?"

"After that first time that we . . . you know," he said, clenching his jaw as he averted his gaze.

"*Why?*"

"Well . . . what you were doing was *dangerous*." Then Mitch fixed on me again, his expression suddenly reproachful. "I wanted to keep a close eye on you to make sure you didn't get up to more stupid, dangerous crap like that." He levelled a glare at me. "I switched stations so I could keep you *safe*, you ungrateful shit."

"I don't even . . . Oh my god, *what* is even happening right now?" I clutched the sides of my head like I could stop my brain from spinning from the outside. "Okay, so let me get this straight . . . in your twisted, psychotic, *fucked up* mind, you were *protecting* me by *raping* me? Is that your logic?" Mitch opened his mouth to answer, but I lifted my hand, stopping him. "No. I call bullshit. I call *bullshit* on all of it. You saw me and fixated on me for some fucking reason. You were in fucking uniform on *purpose* to terrorize me! Were you even on duty that night?"

Mutely, Mitch shook his head.

"*Gahhh*, you fucking *bastard* . . . the whole fucking thing with my fucking license and you threatening to tell my par—" Gritting my teeth, I stared hard at the ceiling for a moment, breathing heavily. "Mitch, you made it your *mission* to rape me and bully me . . . to turn me into"—I gestured to myself helplessly—"this fucking brainwashed idiot who puts up with all your *bullshit!*" I shouted the word.

"Patrick, calm down."

"I will *not* calm down."

"I saw you. I wanted you for myself," Mitch said matter-of-factly, but there was something in his pale blue gaze that was at odds with his confident tone. "And do you forget that I let you go? *I* let *you* go, Patrick." He was silent for a beat, then softly asked, "Why did you want me back if you really think I"—Mitch had the decency to look a little uncomfortable—"*assaulted* you like that?"

I pushed my knuckles into the hollows above my eyes, causing bright stars to erupt against the back of my eyelids, and let out a long sigh. I was suddenly very tired. He couldn't be *that* clueless about what he'd done to me. . . could he? And what about me? What the fuck was *wrong* with me?

"I don't know," I said in all honesty, opening my eyes. "I can't make it make sense."

Mitch sat there saying nothing for a long time. Then, a little wrinkle appeared on his high forehead.

"Does this mean we're not going to Greece?" he asked with a forced, goofy-looking grin.

"Oh my *god*." I couldn't believe he'd joke at a time like this.

"Well, it's a valid question, no?"

I pinched the bridge of my nose. "I'm just trying to wrap my mind around the fact that you've been lying to me and lying to yourself this whole time."

"So . . . we're still going to Greece?"

"Stop that." I scowled at him. "I just want to know one thing: how many other guys did you do your little stalk-and-fuck routine with before you settled on me?"

"What?" Mitch sat upright, looking startled. "*None.*"

"Really?"

"Yeah, *really*."

I tilted my head. "How many people have you fucked since we've been together?"

"We're not together," he replied brusquely. "And, none. Not in the whole six months."

"What about the lady last night?"

"Well, I didn't fuck her, now did I? And I told you I don't want to talk about it."

"Okay," I replied. I didn't know whether to believe him, but he seemed genuinely contrite. "You really don't believe we're a couple?"

"A couple of whats?" he said with a smirk.

I rolled my eyes. "How do you explain to your friends that we live in a one-bedroom apartment?" Then I narrowed my gaze at him pensively. "That's right. You don't *have* friends."

"Well, neither do you," he replied in an even tone.

"I do so . . ."

"Name a single friend you've hung out with in the last month. I'll wait."

"Uh. I hung out with Glenn just last week, remember?"

"Yeah. In a *video game.* Try naming a friend you've actually *met* in real life."

"Online friends *are* real friends."

"Uh-huh, *sure.*" Mitch smirked, but his expression sobered almost immediately. "You're right, though, about friends. I guess that's something we have in common."

"I *have* friends."

"You know what I mean," he replied. "I guess we *are* a couple after all . . . a couple of *losers.*" He said in a lame, jokey voice, then lifted his eyebrows expectantly, his smile strained.

I curled my lip. "Speak for yourself."

Mitch clenched his jaw and blew his breath out slowly through his nose. "Listen, kid, I'm *trying* here."

"Trying *what*, exactly?"

A pained look came over his face. "None of this . . . comes natural to me. I'm not like you. I need . . . time."

"Hey, you know what would help?"

"I swear to god, Patrick, do *not* say therapy."

"Or what? You'll beat me?"

The muscles in Mitch's jaw twitched as he glared at me. Then he let out a slow breath.

"Don't bring therapy up again, please. It's not gonna happen."

Frustrated, I slowly shook my head. "You're fucking impossible, you know that?"

"Deal with it."

"I guess I'm going to have to, aren't I, if we're going to Greece together?"

Mitch's brows shot up in surprise.

I shrugged. Mitch was still the same man who had raped me, but things had . . . *shifted.* It wasn't forgiveness—it was compartmentalization. My future therapy bills would probably bankrupt me.

"I guess it doesn't need to make sense, this thing we have," I said.

His expression softened as his shoulders visibly sagged with relief.

"*C'mere*," he said, beckoning.

I moved my plate from the couch to the coffee table and sat down next to him, putting my head against his chest when he curled his arm around my shoulders. I tucked my hand up under his T-shirt so I could rest it flat against his warm, furry belly as his strong heart thumped against my ear.

"Mitch . . . maybe you really *don't* get it," I said softly. "Maybe you think it was all an act or something, but those first days? You *hurt* me. I lost sleep. I was *terrified*. I felt small and powerless . . . it was like you had ripped away all my self-confidence. I wasn't having a good time, trust me."

Mitch let out a quiet grunt and rested his lips on the top of my head.

"D'you still feel like that?" he murmured into my hair.

"No," I replied, staring into my thoughts. "Weirdly, I feel more confident now than I have in years."

"Hm." I felt him nod. "Weird." After a moment, he cleared his throat. "Patrick? Can I ask you something?"

"Sure."

"Do you still want to get fucked by creepy perverts?"

I laughed. "No. I think I'm good being fucked by just one creepy pervert, thank you."

Mitch's stomach tensed against my palm, and I wondered if I'd gone too far, but he just chuckled. "Fair enough."

"You're thinking about fucking me right now, aren't you?" I asked, staring at the visibly hardening bulge in his sweatpants.

"How can you tell? *Oh.*" Mitch snickered and adjusted himself. "I would, but I don't think I can. My head is fucking killing me."

"I *knew* it."

"Yeah, you're a fucking genius. Good for you, dipshit—you want a medal?" He let out a quiet groan. "Actually, you know what I'd *really* like?"

"What?" I sat up and saw that he had closed his eyes and was rubbing the spot between his brows with his fingertips, wincing.

"I'd like that Advil now."

"Are you sure you don't want to tough it out like a—"

"*Patrick*," Mitch warned.

"—*real* man?" I smiled sweetly at him.

Mitch's hand closed around the back of my neck as he glowered at me—it looked like I might get fucked after all.

I grinned.

CHAPTER 16
GOOD BOY/BAD BOY

"So? Did you have a nice Christmas with your folks?" Mitch asked.

I winced, breathing in sharply. "Can we not talk about my parents while you're trying to put your hand inside me?"

Mitch chuckled. "Thought it would distract you."

Whimpering, I shifted on my knees. "Ow ow ow *ow-ow-ow*! Fuck! That *hurts*. That *hurts*. That *hurts*." It was like a mantra. "Ow . . . *huhhh!*" I let out a ragged breath, sagging as Mitch pulled his hand back a little. I was on my knees, resting forward on my elbows because Mitch had cuffed me to the slatted bedframe when I wouldn't stop pushing him away. I had to hold onto the frame so the metal handcuffs wouldn't bruise my wrists, and my hands were aching from squeezing the wooden slat tight every time he tried to force his fist in.

"*Relax*, Patrick." Mitch put his other hand flat on my lower back. "We've done this like five times now, and it *always* fits. You just have to fucking relax. Okay?"

"It was f-*our*—" My voice hit a high note as Mitch pushed into me hard again. "*Four* times. Not five. *Ow* ohmygod you're going to—ow *ow* fuck *ow*—fucking rip my hole."

"Listen, princess, if it hasn't ripped *yet* . . ." He let out a low, evil laugh at my squeal of pain when his knuckles finally squeezed past my swollen sphincter. "See? You're *fine*. What's that saying about a lady protesting too much?"

I panted, my forehead pressed to the pillow and my eyes clenched shut as my body tensed, struggling to adjust to the hard fist suddenly wrist-deep inside my ass.

"S-speak for yourse—" Gasping, I quickly shook my head as his hand slid further into my throbbing hole. "Stop . . . *stop*! Mitch, please just give me a sec." I breathed out shakily. "*Please*. Just wait a bit."

"All right." Mitch surprised me by softly stroking my sweat-soaked back as he waited for me to recover.

"Oh god," I whispered and licked my lips, lifting myself back up on my elbows. My head was spinning, but the blinding pain in my sphincter and bowels was already fading to a molten, pulsating fullness and my dick was dripping precum onto the sheets. "Just . . . don't go too deep, okay?"

"Fine." Mitch sighed. "Pussy."

I grimaced as his hand began moving slowly inside me. As bad as it hurt getting it *into* me to start with, it was worse when he hit the bend at the top. But as long as he stayed away from the second hole, fisting was something I could tolerate.

Oh fuck. I moaned, shivering as his knuckles raked my prostate. Yeah, maybe I did more than just "tolerate" it. I sucked in a breath through gritted teeth, pushing back gently against him, fucking his fist with my ass for a few thrusts.

"Mmm. Good boy," Mitch said, obviously enjoying himself.

Panting, I wiped my dripping face on my forearm and frowned.

"What do *you* get out of this?" I asked, going still.

"Oh." Mitch was silent for a few seconds, so I looked over my shoulder. His cheeks were pink and his eyes were focused on my ass. "I dunno." He lifted his gaze and gave me a crooked smile when he saw me watching him. "Something about seeing your ass swallow my fist whole is just . . . wild, I guess."

I let out a yelp, then moaned again as he suddenly started fisting me quick and shallow.

"And something about the noises you make," Mitch said, his voice rough with lust. He then let out a quiet snort of laughter. "That is, when you're not hollering and screaming your head off like a little bitch."

"You *like* it when I scream." Breathing hard, I moved my pelvis around in a small circle, turning to face forward again.

"Yeah. Maybe."

"Oh fuck . . . Mitch," I said, desperate. "Can I have one of my hands free? Or . . . can you *please* touch my dick for once?"

Mitch stopped moving. "What? Like . . . jerk you off?"

I nodded quickly and lowered my cheek to the pillow. "You don't have to do it for long. I just . . . I want . . ."

He was still and silent for a long time, then he started pulling his hand out of me.

"Wait wai—" I yelped as his fist popped free with a sharp pain. "Ow. Sorry. Sorry . . . you don't have to. I'm sorry. I shouldn't have asked." But when I raised my head to look back at him again, I saw he was pouring lube into his hands, rubbing them together. He then formed a wedge with his left hand and began shoving it into my ass.

"*Ow*, fuck," I said, but his fist actually went in pretty easy this time. Then, when he grabbed my dick, I realized with excitement that he'd only taken his fist out of me so he could switch and jerk me off properly with his right hand. Mitch almost *never* touched my dick. However, my eyes popped open in alarm a second later.

"*Hey*, not so hard."

"You wanted me to jerk you off? You're getting jerked off," he growled and began giving me the most *aggressive* hand job of my life. He stroked my cock too hard and fast, his fist like a vise clamped around my shaft while punching my insides with the other hand.

I came so quickly that I didn't have time to breathe in—instead of a yell, I gave a weird guttural cough, then inhaled with an overly loud gasp, like I had almost suffocated . . . and *then* I yelled. My dick virtually exploded onto the bed beneath me, drenching the already precum-covered sheet, the force of my climax pushing Mitch's hand out of my ass so violently I barely felt it.

As I drooped there, clinging to the bedframe and fighting for breath in the aftermath of my orgasm, I heard Mitch grunt. His cum splashed against the burning, stretched-out rim of my ass, dripping inside me and off my balls as he aimed for my wide-open hole.

"Fuck," he rasped, making the bed jiggle as he moved forward, suddenly shoving his cock inside me to milk the last of his cum directly into my guts. Then he collapsed on his side and lay there with his eyes closed, a blissful smile on his face. "Oh yeah."

"Mitch?"

His lids slowly lifted, and he turned to me, his gaze unfocused. "What?"

"Can you do something about these before you pass out?" I jangled the cuffs against the wooden slat.

"No." He shut his eyes again.

"*What?*"

Mitch sat up with a grin. "Kidding. I'm kidding." He wiped his hands on the sheets and grabbed the key from the bedstand. "There you go." After freeing me, he stretched out on his back on the dry side of the bed, his hands laced behind his head.

I rubbed my sore wrists with numb fingers for a moment before gingerly crawling backwards out of the mess and off the bed.

"*Please* tell me that's the last time today," I said in a croaky voice as I stood there unsteadily. My wrecked sphincter throbbed, burning like it was literally on fire, and cum leaked out of me in thick pulses as my ass kept clenching and releasing involuntarily in response to the abuse Mitch had put it through. My hole felt so swollen it was like I was holding a ball between my ass cheeks.

"We'll see."

I groaned softly.

Mitch had arrived home that afternoon, finally back from visiting his mom in Florida for the holidays, and he'd been on me inside of a minute. Not even bothering with a hello, he'd bent me over the dining table to fuck me like he'd been gone a month instead of six days. Then he'd had me a second time before his dick had even had a chance to dry. I think someone missed me—or, at least, missed my ass.

"Uh," I said, scratching the back of my head. "Mitch?"

"*What?*"

"I should put the sheets in the laundry before things . . . you know, set."

Mitch sighed, but he sat up. "Well, at least you're turning into a good little housewife," he said, swinging his legs off the side of the bed. "Empty my bag and wash that stuff too, while you're at it."

"Okay." I waited until he left for the bathroom to start stripping the bed. Then I dutifully opened his duffel bag and dumped it out on the floor, separating out his dirty laundry from his baseball cap and toiletry kit . . . then stopped and sat back on my heels when I found a gift-wrapped package.

"Go on," Mitch said, startling me. "It's for you. Open it."

I glanced back and saw he was leaning against the doorframe, his arms crossed, watching me with a small smile.

"Oh. Okay." Feeling a mix of giddiness and dread—because who the fuck knew what kind of gift Mitch would give me—I peeled the tape off the green-and-gold Christmas paper. Inside was a small box, and in the box was a Switch game cartridge with some Chinese characters on it and nothing else. I looked to Mitch for an explanation, my eyes wide.

"So, it's by the same company that made that stupid game you play all the time. It's not out yet—it's actually still in development—but my buddy assured me that it's playable."

A new game by the makers of *Genshin*? I blinked rapidly as I stared at the game cartridge. I was so surprised and confused.

I frowned. "Like a bootleg?"

Mitch chuckled and shook his head. "No. It's a—whatchamacallit—an early build? From the company. And . . . uh, you get to test it for them or some shit. You gotta sign an NDA, though. The info is in the box."

"But . . . how?" I said in a faint voice, lifting my eyes back to Mitch.

He shrugged. "I know a guy who knows a guy."

"Oh my god." I sprang to my feet and threw myself at Mitch, wrapping my arms around his neck to kiss him. "I *love* it. Thank you. *Thank* you."

"Yeah, well, you're welcome," he said gruffly. I knew he was trying to look all nonchalant about it, but I could see he was pleased that he'd made me happy.

I went to kiss him again and then froze, dismayed. "I, uh . . . I got you something too but it's *so* lame compared to this."

"Whatever." Mitch gave another shrug. "I don't need anything."

"Hang on." I pulled away from him and quickly went to the closet. I found the gift bag I had hidden there. "Well . . . if you don't like it, I'll get you something better." I held it out to him, feeling like a cheap asshole.

"It's fine." He took the bag and looked inside, then frowned, pulling out the small package. "What is it?"

"It's a new Bluetooth adapter for your car. Oh . . . and look"—I pointed to the different features, getting excited despite myself—"you can answer a call with a touch, it has *twice* the range . . . and, you can charge your phone here, and the best part is that it's guaranteed not to cut out if you've got your phone in your pocket. Oh, and it has good bass. Supposedly."

A genuine smile slowly creased Mitch's handsome face before he caught himself and squared his expression, nodding brusquely. "It's good. Thanks." He looked closer at the adapter. "It's a good gift . . . I just hope you didn't spend too much."

I rolled my eyes and went up on tiptoe to plant another kiss on his lips. This time, he curled his free arm around my waist and kissed me back, showing his appreciation in a way he still couldn't bring himself to do with words. He was an emotionally constipated asshole . . . but he was *my* emotionally constipated asshole.

Too soon, he pulled back and gave me a stern look.

"Okay, enough of that. Get the laundry done, and then you're allowed to play your game for a bit. Not all night . . . an hour max. Got it?"

I nodded. "Okay. Thank you."

His expression gentled, and he pinched my chin between thumb and forefinger.

"Good boy."

The thrill I felt when he used those words hadn't diminished in the slightest. If anything, they touched me deeper every time he said them.

After supper, Mitch and I settled on the couch to watch something, but after only a few minutes, he shifted away from me and unbuckled his belt.

"Um. What are you doing?" I asked quietly, watching him unzip his fly. I stared in dismay as he pulled his hard cock out. Mitch's libido was frightening.

"Come here and sit on my dick," he said with a grin.

I shook my head. "I *can't*, Mitch."

Frowning, he grabbed me by the back of the neck and squeezed hard, pulling me towards him.

"Please," I gasped, shoving at his chest. "Mitch . . . Mitch *stop*. I'm serious."

"So"—Mitch grunted, tugging on my sweatpants as he

grappled with me—"am I. Will you stop that? Jesus." He yanked my arm behind my back, causing me to tumble against him so that my shoulder wouldn't dislocate.

"*Fuck*. Mitch, please please please . . ." I whispered against his chest as he wrestled my pants down. My tears soaked into his T-shirt. "I'm so sore. I can't. Please. If you this . . . just . . . just knock me out first or something."

Mitch froze, his grip on my wrist loosening. "*What?*"

I lifted my head and stared at him tearfully. "My ass is so sore . . . I don't think I could handle it if you fucked me right now. I'm literally piss-myself-scared of how much it'll hurt."

His brows slowly pinched together as he studied my face.

"What—what if I used my mouth? You've never really given me a chance to try again." I smiled at him, wiping at my tears. "C'mon . . . let me give you a nice blow job? Please?"

Mitch's mouth twisted to the side as he mulled over my request. He liked hurting me, *loved* when I was in pain, but maybe there was a limit to that after all.

"All right," he said, releasing me.

Gratefully, I slid off the couch and kneeled between his thighs. I blinked up at him nervously.

"But . . . just let me do my thing, okay? Don't grab my head and try to force yourself down my throat . . . please?"

He chuckled and lifted his hands, palms out. "I won't touch. Promise," he said, stretching his arms out to either side to rest them on the back of the couch. "Go on. Suck my cock."

I licked my lips, staring at his massively thick cock, then laughed inwardly. I was all jittery like I was about to give my first blow job, which was ridiculous. I'd sucked a *lot* of dick in my life. Squaring my shoulders, I took Mitch's shaft in both hands, then rose up and slowly licked around his crown, ending with my tongue in his slit.

Mitch sighed and I lifted my eyes to his.

"If that's what you're going to do . . . I'd rather *oh*—" His brow creased and lips parted as I took his cockhead in my mouth, my tongue pushing into his frenulum as I sucked to exert pressure. I slid my hands down his shaft and widened my jaw to take in a little more of his cock, careful not to go too far or I would gag, and swirled my tongue as I went, then reversed course and focused on his head as my hands came back up so that I was both jerking him off and blowing him at the same time.

It was nothing fancy, but I knew Mitch was enjoying it because he let out a quiet moan, shifting his hips with my movements as I stroked and sucked his spit-covered cock, eagerly lapping up the precum from his slit as I went.

"Okay, that's not bad," Mitch said, his voice a little hoarse.

"Mm?" I replied gratefully, gazing up at him with my mouth full.

"Oh yeah. Keep looking at me like that." Mitch exhaled slowly, his eyes growing heavy-lidded and cheeks pinkening as he watched me work on his dick. "Fuck, yeah. Jesus, Patrick, you look good with my cock in your mouth."

I hummed again, smiling with my eyes as I picked up the pace, struggling to swallow as his precum started running down the back of my throat.

Mitch broke his promise not to touch, but it was just to hold my head between his hands lightly, not shove me down like he had that first time. His fingers dug into my scalp gently as he began to huff out his breaths.

"Play with my balls," he gasped out, his hips thrusting a little faster.

Cupping his sack in one hand, I gingerly squeezed his nuts, and his dick jerked in response.

"Yeah. Harder."

I obliged, and he let out a deep moan, shutting his eyes to lean his head back on the couch. Though I was enjoying myself, I had no idea how close he was and my jaw was getting sore, so I thought maybe a little more stimulation might bring him over the edge. I quickly licked my finger to wet it, then cupped his balls again, but this time, I extended my finger to touch his pucker.

Mitch immediately jerked his knees together and sat up. Thankfully, I spat out his cock as he clamped me tight between his thighs. Otherwise, I might have accidentally bitten him.

"What the fuck was that?" he rasped, staring wild-eyed at me, his chest heaving.

"I was just goin—"

"That is *exit only*, Patrick."

"But—"

"You try that again and I will permanently *damage* you." He tightened his grip on my head, squeezing painfully.

I gaped up at him, my heart pounding.

"I'm . . . um, I'm sorry," I stammered, frankly terrified by the outrage twisting his features. "I'm sorry, Mitch. I shouldn't have done that. That was stupid of me. That was dumb. Really, *really* dumb. I won't do it again. I promise."

Mitch's expression thawed as I babbled, and he stopped trying to crush my head, apparently mollified by my apology. He dropped his hands, frowning as he averted his gaze. I might have been imagining things, but Mitch seemed a little embarrassed by how he'd reacted.

"Um. Do you want me to continue?" I asked quietly, glancing down at his half-hard cock.

"Nah," Mitch replied dismissively. "I'm not in the fucking mood." He quickly tucked himself back into his pants and stood up, causing me to fall back on my ass as he zipped his fly. "Going to bed."

Shit. "Okay," I said in a small voice. "Do you want me to come wi—"

"I don't care."

Tears blurred my vision as I watched him stalk off to the bedroom.

CHAPTER 17
SLAPPED ASS

"Fucking hell, Patrick," Mitch said suddenly. "Can you *stop* that?"

I blinked at him a few times, my pulse surging. "Stop what?" I'd been tidying up the apartment while he watched TV.

"Stop walking around with a face like a slapped ass."

I lifted my brows, staring at him in confusion.

Mitch sighed and sat up, hitting mute on the remote. "You've been walking around all week looking like a beaten dog."

"Oh."

"It's annoying. Stop it."

"Oh. Sorry," I replied, shoving my hands into my pockets. I'd been walking on eggshells around Mitch since the "exit only" incident, as I'd taken to thinking of it. "I just feel bad about what happened the other day."

Mitch levelled his gaze at me. "Listen. *Nothing* happened the other day," he said evenly.

"*Oh.*" The tightness in my chest immediately released—apparently, I was forgiven.

"And stop saying 'oh'. You sound like a fucking idiot."

"Sorry."

"*Jesus*, Patrick." Mitch exhaled and closed his eyes, rubbing the spot between his brows in a tired sort of way. "You're killing me."

"Um—"

"If another 'sorry' comes out of your mouth, I'm going to put you over my knee."

My eyes widened.

He chuckled. "Yeah, you know what? I really should give you that spanking you ought to have gotten as a kid."

Spanking? I just stood there, extremely conscious of the fact that my dick had gone from zero to rock hard in seconds, wondering what to say. I hadn't gotten off in days—despite what had happened, Mitch hadn't stopped fucking me, but I'd been too anxious to enjoy it.

Mitch narrowed his eyes, giving me a pointed look like he was waiting for something.

Oh. I laughed nervously. "I'm . . . *sorry.*"

"That's it," Mitch said with an unconvincing growl in his voice. "Come here."

He had me drop my pants and, after teasing me about my erection, made me lie across his lap, consequently winding up with my dick squeezed between his thighs. Stroking my backside softly, Mitch chuckled to himself.

"Oh, I'm going to enjoy this," he said. His hand stopped moving. "Wait, has *anyone* ever spanked you?"

I thought about how some guys liked to slap my ass while fucking me, but I didn't think that counted, so I shook my head.

"*No?*" Mitch's laugh was sinister as he lifted his hand. "You're not going to be able to sit for *days*," he said, punctuating the word with a sharp smack to my backside.

I yelled out in pain and alarm, wondering if I was going to regret this as Mitch landed a few more blows to my ass, each harder than the last. "*Ow.*"

"I'm just getting started, sunshine."

"Oh god."

. . .

Mitch kept hitting me, sometimes on the same cheek over and over until I was sobbing and shaking so hard my teeth chattered. Then he would switch and start slapping the backs of my thighs as my ass throbbed in time to my heartbeat. My skin was on *fire*.

"Ow! Mit . . .*uff* . . . Mitch, not so ha—" I yelped as he went back to beating my ass cheeks. "Not so h-hard," I begged in a broken voice.

"*Wah*. Not so hard," he repeated in a squeaky voice, mocking me. "This is *nothing*." He smacked the same spot rapidly until I was screaming with every breath, then he stopped to run his palm gently over my blistering skin. Even *that* hurt.

I panted, my eyes shut tight, then I yelled out when Mitch suddenly dug between my legs and pulled my balls back, anchoring them there behind my thighs.

"Oh my god. Oh no. No no *no*," I pleaded as I craned my head to look at him.

With a wide grin, Mitch landed a stinging slap to my ass, right above where my balls were trapped, and I sagged in relief, thinking I had mistaken his intent. However, the next blow landed on my sack—just the tips of his fingers and not half as hard as he had been hitting me up until now, but sharp enough that it forced all the air from my lungs with a high-pitched squeal.

"Oh, I *liked* that," Mitch said in a husky voice. The whole time he'd been hitting me, his hard dick was like a rock against my hip. "Let's see if you'll do it again." He whacked my nuts again, and I cried out, my hands clawing the couch cushion as if I could drag myself off his lap to escape.

I couldn't, though, not with my dick crushed between his legs.

Bawling so hard I could barely breathe, I suffered through another round of ringing smacks to my ass before he gave my balls one final sharp thwack with his fingertips. Then he shoved the coffee table back and pushed me off his lap onto the floor, where I landed with a jarring thump.

Quickly pinning me beneath him, Mitch spat in his hand and fed his cock into my ass, ramming it in deep as I cried out. He began thrusting hard and fast but lasted only a few seconds before he stilled and grunted, flooding my hole with cum.

"Oh fuck," he said, panting. "Jesus."

Then Mitch surprised me by pulling out almost immediately. Yanking me by the hips, he lifted me to my hands and knees.

"What are you . . . *uhh*—" I inhaled quickly, dropping my head with a moan as he wrapped one hand around my swollen cock and shoved a finger into my cum-slick hole.

Mitch began rapidly jerking me off while stroking my prostate, making me gasp and shudder as he quickly brought me to the brink.

"Oh oh *oh* fuck oh *fuck*," I whispered, my thighs trembling as my balls tightened. "I'm gonna cum."

Mitch chuckled. "Go ahead. You've earned it," he said and slipped a second finger into me.

I breathed in sharply through clenched teeth, my hips jerking of their own volition, then let loose with a long, sobbing wail as the first pulse hit. Cum hit the floor with an audible *splat*, and I grunted and whimpered as I emptied myself, my climax pulsing from so deep in my core that I felt like I was being pulled inside out by pleasure. Chest heaving, I crushed my eyes closed and let out one last hoarse moan, then yelped as Mitch's probing touch became too intense for my sensitive, throbbing hole. I lurched forward to escape and wound up collapsing on my stomach in the cooling puddle.

Mitch snorted in amusement and I grinned dazedly, rising onto my hands and knees again. But that's as far as I got—there was no strength left in my legs to stand, so I just stayed there swaying and shaking and giggling in that heightened state of bliss where my laughter could turn into tears at any second.

"Jesus," Mitch said with a laugh. "Okay, enough of that, Patrick." He stood and scooped me up. I winced and yelped, but he adjusted his hold to avoid the worst of my bruises and I sighed, resting my head against his shoulder as he carried me in his arms to the bedroom.

Mitch set me down carefully on my side on the duvet and I beamed up at him blearily.

"Seems like you enjoyed yourself, eh?" he said with a smirk. "Well, I guess I'll go get some ice for that backside of yours." He turned to leave, but I grabbed his wrist.

"You know that's all I was trying to do," I said. "The other day. You know . . . with the finger. I just wanted to make you feel good."

Mitch's brows came together and his lips pressed into a hard line. Then he exhaled through his nose and his expression softened.

"Yeah. I know," was all he said. Then he left the room.

CHAPTER 18
PÉCHÉ SACRÉ

MARCH

I chewed quickly, carefully keeping my face neutral as I ate—then I swallowed, paused to suppress a shudder, and took another bite of my omelette. Mitch insisted that I eat vegetables at every meal, and usually that was all right, but I *hated* bell peppers. Flaring my nostrils, I quickly choked down another bite and winced, shifting in my seat. I had to pee *so* bad.

Mitch looked up from the news article he was reading and frowned.

"Sit up," he said. "What's the matter with you?"

"It's nothing," I replied, forcing myself to sit still.

He levelled a stony look at me.

I sighed. "I have to pee."

"Really?" Mitch shook his head disgustedly, then took a sip of his coffee. "You can't hold it? What are you, a child?"

"No, but . . . I *really* gotta go."

"What do you say, then?"

"May I please be excused?" I asked quietly. I'd had to finish my meals in wet pants before, which was pretty awful . . . but the showers with Mitch afterwards *were* nice.

"Fine."

"Thank you." I popped up and ran to the bathroom to relieve my near-to-bursting bladder. Afterwards, I washed my hands and smiled at my reflection. I might have hated some of the stuff Mitch forced me to eat, but he'd been right about the benefits of a better diet. I'd put on enough weight that my face no longer looked so hollow, and my skin looked nicer. Even my hair, which had always been sort of dull and floppy, was now glossy and brighter blond, and when I swept it back from my forehead, I thought it looked pretty nice. I cocked my head, my grin deepening. However, eating healthy wasn't the only thing that was having a positive effect on me. Being with Mitch was just . . . *so*—

Blinking out of my reverie, I realized I was keeping Mitch waiting and hurried out of the bathroom. I was confused when I saw he had moved my half-finished breakfast in front of him, wondering if he meant to eat it himself, and then saw he had pulled his cock out and was stroking it as he read.

"Uh . . ."

Mitch looked up from his tablet and stared at me expectantly.

I stood there for a beat, then noticed the bottle of lube on the table.

"*Oh.*" I dutifully dropped my shorts, greased up my hole, and swung a leg over his thighs to straddle him, facing away. Easing myself down onto his hard cock, I whimpered softly, my insides still sore from the early morning pounding I'd taken, then sighed happily as I settled. As I resumed my breakfast impaled on Mitch's lap, he slipped one hand up the front of my T-shirt to idly play with my nipples while he read.

Somehow, the bell peppers didn't taste so bad anymore.

. . .

When I was done eating, Mitch set aside his tablet and simply grabbed me around the waist as he stood, then bent me over the table to fuck me with long, slow thrusts that forced deep moans out of me every time my hole was fully stretched out by his thick cock.

Soon, I was skirting the edge, clutching onto the table, chest heaving and eyes shut as my body tensed for release. I was *right* at the cusp . . . and then Mitch abruptly pulled out his cock and shot his load all over my ass and lower back. I glanced over my shoulder and watched him jerk the last few drops onto me, then frowned in dismay as he zipped up his pants and buckled his belt.

"*Hey*," I croaked, my gaping hole constricting and releasing rhythmically a few times in reaction to being abandoned so suddenly. "What are you doing?" I pushed myself up on arms made of noodles. "What about *me*?"

"What *about* you?"

Disappointed and confused, I stood up and turned around, crossing my arms over my chest, my sad little boner already drooping. He normally didn't just *stop*—I think he secretly enjoyed my orgasms almost as much as I did—but when he *did* stop, it was usually because I had annoyed him. Or, annoyed him *more* than usual.

"Is it because I asked to go pee?" I asked in a meek voice.

Mitch laughed at my expression and reached out to cup my face with one hand.

"Don't worry, sunshine. I'll let you empty your balls . . . *later*." He slapped my cheek lightly. "After you've done the dishes and swept, you can play your game for a bit, but this afternoon, I want you to wash yourself *really* well—inside and out. I mean it. I *really* want that pussy to sparkle."

I frowned. "Uh. Okay?"

"And take some extra time with shaving. I want you *smooth* as a baby's ass."

"Everywhere or . . ."

"Your face, your chest, your nutsack, and your ass." He reached around and gave my backside a hard squeeze.

"*Ow*. Okay. Not my legs or armpits?"

He shook his head, sliding his hand along the underside of my ass cheek until he reached my hole. I whimpered as he gave me a quick, shallow fingering that brought my cock back to life, then sighed as he pulled out. He scooped up some of the cum running down my crack and lifted his fingers to my lips. I opened my mouth, dutifully cleaning off his fingers as he gazed down at me with an oddly subdued expression.

"Good boy," he murmured.

I grinned.

I stared out the window of the Corolla, my brow furrowed as I watched the streetlights shimmering in the rain. We were driving east toward downtown, but Mitch hadn't said where we were going, and I was afraid I'd get my head bitten off if I asked. He'd been dismissive and insulting all afternoon, his temper steadily getting shorter as the day wore on—though whatever was bothering him didn't seem to be my fault. If I didn't know any better, I would say Mitch was nervous about something. But what the hell could make Mitch nervous?

I chewed on the side of my thumb, trying to guess where he was taking me.

"Get your fingers out of your mouth," Mitch growled.

"Sorry." I folded my hands in my lap and glanced over. Mitch was hunched over the steering wheel, squinting through the streaks his shitty wipers left on the windshield and driving *way* too fast like usual. I winced as he cut across two lanes to take the next exit, my heart leaping into my throat when the tires briefly lost their grip on the road. Terrifyingly, we hydroplaned several meters before Mitch regained control of the car.

"Jesus," I whispered, my mouth dry.

Mitch tapped the brakes hard at the next intersection, jerking me forward hard against my seatbelt, then took a sharp left.

"Are we . . . late for something?" I asked quietly.

Mitch shook his head. "Not yet."

"All right." I craned my neck to see the street signs as we whizzed by and realized we were on René-Lévesque heading east. At the next intersection, Mitch turned left again and recognized the area instantly. *Huh.* I turned to Mitch and studied his expression. "This is the Village."

"Yep," Mitch said, taking a little side street and almost colliding with an empty BIXI stand on the next street. He zigzagged through the next few streets and then abruptly stopped next to a low, blocky office building that housed a dentist, a pharmacy, a graphic design company, a travel agency, and some kind of tech company, judging by the name of it. Mitch opened the door and ducked out into the rain, opening the back door to grab his duffel bag. "Let's go."

I followed him out and pulled my jacket up over my head to shield me from the deluge, completely confused as he led us to the office building. He held the door open for me, then went to the intercom system beneath the directory of businesses, keyed in some numbers, and waited. Were we booking our trip to Greece? I looked at the code next to the travel agency, but it didn't match the numbers Mitch had entered.

The intercom crackled to life. "*Oui?*"

"*Chu dans marde,*" Mitch replied cryptically.

Alarmed, I just stared at him. Why was he saying he was in trouble? A second later, the inner door buzzed, and Mitch yanked it open. I nervously followed him down the dark, marbled hallway and stepped into the elevator. When Mitch hit the basement button, my fear got the better of me.

"Mitch, where are we going? What the hell is going on?" I asked, my heart pounding.

Mitch turned to me and smiled for the first time all afternoon when he saw my expression. "Relax," he said, then he took my hand.

I swallowed and nodded. There was a tightness to his expression that still worried me, but the fact that he was holding hands with me was just . . . confounding. I couldn't decide whether I should be *more* scared or less because of it.

The elevator door opened and Mitch led me down a narrow corridor. Soon, I could hear music. At the end of the hallway, we came to a pink door and stopped. Mitch knocked.

After a moment, the door opened and revealed a tall bald man in a black suit. He saw Mitch and visibly tensed. "Officer," he said curtly, his nostrils flaring. The suit was so tight on his broad shoulders that it seemed like the seams would give at any moment. It creaked when he moved.

"Dylan," Mitch replied evenly.

"I'd say it was nice to see you again, but I'd be lying," Dylan replied. His thick brows rose when he noticed me standing next to Mitch. "Hello, there."

"Hi," I replied quietly.

"So?" Mitch said impatiently.

Dylan rolled his eyes then opened the door wider, bowing at the waist with a flourish as he pulled a dark velvet curtain aside. "Welcome to Le Péché Sacré."

Wide-eyed, I pushed past the curtain into a crazy graffitied hallway lit by bright pink, heart-shaped wall sconces. The music I had heard earlier was coming from somewhere to my left, and to my right were a series of doors with glittering door frames.

"Where *are* we?" I asked, blinking rapidly as I watched a man in six-inch heels and a thong walk past with a bottle of champagne and glasses on a silver tray.

Mitch didn't reply; he just dragged me down the hallway to the second door, which led to a shorter corridor. He tried the first door, but it was locked. When the second door he tried opened, I saw it was a little room with clothing hooks on the wall and a full-length mirror, like a changing room.

"Mitch?" My heart was in my throat. "What the hell is going on?"

Mitch thrust a small blue bag at me, his jaw muscles bulging as he stared at me for a moment. "Put this on. And be quick about it."

"What?" I clutched the bag, whimpering when he shoved me into the changing room and shut the door behind me. I stood there in a daze for a second, then pulled the bag's drawstring with numb fingers. The first item I pulled out was a little bra made of filmy white netting. I stared at it in dismay. Why would Mitch think I'd want to wear something like it? Never in my life had I had any desire to wear anything remotely feminine. "You've got to be kidding me," I whispered. Nevertheless, I stripped off my shirt and dutifully put on the bra, struggling with the little clasp in the back until I realized I could put it on backwards and just turn it around. Next, I fished out what was apparently the panties, except it was just a waistband with a triangle of white netting sewed to it, and though there was a little loop on the other end of the triangle, I could see no way of attaching it to the waistband. Confused, I looked into the bag again and saw something silvery at the bottom. I dug out a small metal butt plug with a plain circular base. *What the hell?* There was also a small tube of lubricant and a pair of soft white ballet-type slippers in the bag . . . and that was it. No instructions. Then I realized the loop at the end of the triangle was elastic and a lightbulb went off in my head. I took off my pants, stepped into the waistband of the underwear and worked the plug through the loop on the triangle before pulling it back between my legs. Then I swore, realizing I'd forgotten the lube. Once my hole was prepped, the cold plug slid in easily, anchoring the panties in place. I turned and looked at myself in the mirror and made a face.

"Patrick?" Mitch said, knocking on the door. "What the fuck is taking so long?"

"I look like an idiot," I yelled back.

"Get out here."

Sighing, I quickly put on the stretchy, soft slippers, gathered up my things, and opened the door. Mitch took my clothes and boots, stuffing them into his duffel, then stepped back to appraise my ridiculous outfit. When he tilted his head and frowned, I could tell he was disappointed. I folded my arms, embarrassed. After a second, he sighed and grabbed me by the wrist.

"C'mon."

Mitch pulled me back the way we had come and turned down a different hall. This place, Le Péché Sacré was *huge* . . . but what *was* it? The name meant "sacred sin" . . . but was it a dance club? Or, judging from my outfit, some sort of . . . kinky burlesque . . . something? I stared wide-eyed at a group of men who passed us wearing only jockstraps and boots. "Uh . . . Mitch?"

Mitch abruptly stopped in front of a door covered in shiny palm tree decorations and pushed it open. On the other side was a large dressing room with tables and mirrors to either side. In the middle were wheeled clothing racks bursting with feathers, sequins, leather, and latex. A lone drag queen sat in front of one of the mirrors, the makeup brush paused an inch from her cheek. She stared at us for a few long seconds in the mirror's reflection, her icy gaze putting Mitch's to shame.

"Officer Mitch," she said curtly, setting down the brush. She slowly rose to her feet and I could only gaze up in wonder. The word that came to mind was "glorious".

The drag queen had bright ginger curls piled high on her head, decorated with a large, glittering green hairpin in the shape of a dragonfly. Her makeup was dramatic yet sophisticated, and she had a beard with a sleek, upwards-curled moustache—both were a rich, mahogany red. She wore a silvery gown with a plunging neckline that framed her densely furred torso all the way down to her pubic bone, and her belly button was pierced with a jewelled ring that matched the emeralds adorning her hairpin and swaying chandelier earrings. She was like a gorgeous, towering, bearded version of that classic Barbie doll. I realized my mouth was hanging open and shut it, then smiled nervously when she turned her luminous green eyes on me.

"Well, hello there," she said softly. "And who are you, honey?"

"Patrick," I replied, sounding slightly hoarse, and reflexively held my hand out to shake . . . which I instantly felt stupid for doing. *What am I doing?*

However, the drag queen took my hand in hers, and instead of shaking, she turned it over and lifted it to her lips, pressing a light kiss to my knuckles. She smiled. "*Enchanté.*"

The laugh that came out of me was weird and squeaky.

"Well? Can you fix this?" Mitch snapped.

"Fix *what?*" she replied, her eyes narrowing to slits as she stared down at him.

"Make him . . . I don't know. Prettier?"

The drag queen raised her brows slowly. "I can. But what's the magic word?"

The muscles rolled in Mitch's jaw, and he huffed out an audible breath through his nose.

"Can you *please*, make Patrick prettier?" he finally asked in a restrained tone.

"That's better," she replied.

"Good," Mitch replied, then left the room without another word.

"Come here, honey," the drag queen said, drawing back the chair she had only just vacated.

I sat down, crossing my arms over my chest to hold my elbows.

"I'm Daquiri Bollivard by the way," she said with a friendly smile. "But you can call me Dee."

Daquiri Bollivard? Why did that sound familiar? I snorted and grinned up at her. "Like Décarie Boulevard?" I asked, amused.

Dee nodded, her grin crooking up to one side and deepening the dimple there. "*Exactly.*"

"Are you from NDG?"

Laughing, Dee nodded again. "Born and raised, baby."

Suddenly, it felt a little easier to breathe around her. I blinked. Oops. *Her?*

"Um. What are your pronouns?" I asked.

"How sweet of you to ask," Dee replied. "Well, it's 'him' or 'they' if you see me on the street, and 'they' or 'she' when my face is this beat." They made an elegant little pose with one hand resting on their cheek like they were a fifties starlet. Dee then narrowed their eyes at me. "What about you, honey?"

"Oh," I laughed, shrugging, "plain old 'him' for me."

"All right." Dee turned to pick through a case full of makeup and brushes. "But your daddy wants you to look *pretty*," they said, lining up a few small things of makeup on the table. Dee turned to me, their expression pensive. "How do you feel about that?"

"Well, um, he's not my daddy and it's not a good idea to use that word around him."

Dee quirked an eyebrow in response.

"Yeah, it's a whole thing. But, um . . . I don't know? I've never worn anything like this." I looked down and shook my head. "Or makeup." I sighed, feeling self-conscious.

"Do you *want* to?"

"Not really. But Mitch wants me to."

"I see. I'm just trying to make sure Officer Mitch isn't bullying you into something you don't want to do," Dee said gently.

"*Oh*. Oh no, it's fine. If it makes him happy, that's what I want."

"Okay, so it *is* that sort of dynamic." Dee's smile returned. "As long as he's not *forcing* you."

"Well . . ." I grinned sheepishly. "That's part of the appeal."

Dee's eyes widened, then they chuckled and shook their head, picking up a bottle of something from the table. "All right. If it makes you happy, then that's what counts." They wrinkled their nose at me. "Look at me being such a busybody." They sighed. "All right, let's make you pretty."

Dee started applying things to my face, mostly creams and powders that were faintly perfumed, and I wondered if they would make me look extravagant or gaudy. I hoped not. I didn't think either would look good on me, and something told me Mitch wouldn't think so either.

"Um," I said after clearing my throat. "So . . . Mitch has been here before?"

"Yeah," Dee replied with a small grimace.

"But, what *is* this place?"

Dee straightened, looking surprised. "Oh, well, we're a private club. A mix of this and that. There's dancing space, two bars, a stage . . ."

"Yeah, but what *kind* of club? What happens here?"

Grinning like the Cheshire cat, Dee answered, "Sex, honey. *Sex* happens."

"Oh." My pulse ticked up again and I felt my stomach clench. Was Mitch planning on pimping me out to people in the club?

Dee studied my expression as they resumed applying makeup to my face. "We do technically cater to everyone—gay, straight, and everyone in between, but the clientele is largely queer and leaning male. There are glory holes and no-holes-barred rooms, sex shows and a sauna . . . a dungeon and erotic massages. We even have some old-school coin-operated peepshow booths, the kind where you put in a penny to raise the curtain for two minutes while someone does a little erotic dance for you—though, they're a loonie these days instead of a penny. But, if it involves sex . . . you can find it here."

"Huh." I furrowed my brow. "What do you do?"

"I'm one of the six owners and emcee three times a week. I also do a little sing and dance number later, if you want to stay and watch . . . sexy but not *sex*. Just fun." Dee tilted their head with a thoughtful expression as they touched a brush to the tip of my nose.

"Um. You wouldn't happen to know why I'm here, would you?"

"Officer Mitch paid for a slot of stage time. I'm guessing it's going to be a show with you. Other than that, I don't know."

I looked down at myself. I could see my limp cock through the sheer panties and was suddenly very aware of the butt plug lodged inside me when my hole gave a little spasm. I was excited *and* terrified. "Okay."

"Keep your head like this," Dee said, raising my chin with one of their sharp-nailed fingers.

"Sorry." I kept as still as possible. "So, how long has he been coming here? A little under a year, right?" I figured this is where Mitch started going after his marriage with Nour broke down . . . right around when he started stalking me.

"No, it was . . ." Dee paused in their application of something on my cheek and wrinkled their brow delicately, thinking. "I think it was two or three years ago that Officer Mitch and his goons stormed the place." Dee resumed working as they talked. "Someone had called in an anonymous tip that there was underage sex taking place at Péché Sacré, and they closed us down. It was nonsense, of course, but that didn't stop them from ripping the place apart while they interrogated us. They found nothing and we opened back up a few days later. Then, maybe a month went by, and look at that . . . there's Officer Mitch at the door. Not in uniform, but who can forget a face like his—*especially* if you were grilled by him until the crack of fuck in the morning." Dee's nostrils flared as they shook their head, looking angry. "But what can you do? *Not* let him in? One phone call and he could get us shut down again for some bullshit. So we decided to allow him into the club."

I had no doubt that it was *exactly* the sort of thing Mitch would have done . . . he'd done it to me, hadn't he? He was all about entering uninvited.

"And was it okay? What did he do?"

"He was polite. Quiet. Went and sat at the bar near the stage and ordered a few drinks. Tipped well. Made no fuss . . . just watched a few shows and left. Then, a week later, there he was again. Same thing—a few quiet drinks, good tips, and gone. But his presence sets *everyone* on edge. Some of the staff refuse to work on nights he's here." Dee smirked, doing something to my eyebrows. "His shirts *did* get a bit tighter over time . . . with an extra button undone and the sleeves rolled up in that sexy way. A little cologne. Eyes that started wandering." Straightening, Dee examined their work. "And then one week, he didn't show. And the week after that. So, we thought we were free of his presence . . . but here we are again. I nearly choked on my chai earlier when I saw him on the roster."

I listened in a daze, trying to picture Mitch coming to a place like this week after week.

"He stopped coming last summer?"

Dee nodded. "That's right, honey. Why?"

"That's when he— That's when we met."

"Ah. Interesting." Dee smiled at me. "I always got the sense that he was looking for something specific. I guess that something was *you*."

I glanced down. My ears were suddenly hot and the flutter in my chest was making it hard to breathe.

Chuckling, Dee brushed my hair back and lifted my chin again to gaze down at me with warmth as they studied my face.

"Huh," was all they said with a soft smile.

I cleared my throat and scratched the back of my neck as I lifted one shoulder in a shrug.

"Uh. Um. Hey, so when you talked about him just now, it sounded like you actually sort of like him—"

Dee's eyes went wide with affront. "I do *not* like Officer Mitch. I merely tolerate him."

"Oh, I tolerate you too, Dee."

At the sound of Mitch's voice, I turned and froze, openly gawking at him.

"Oh my," Dee said quietly.

Mitch looked like he could have stepped right out of a Tom of

Finland comic. He wore a black leather bulldog harness over his bare chest and tight-fitting black leather pants that accentuated his significant bulge. He wore his regular black work boots—but they had been shined—some fingerless black motorcycle gloves, and his cop hat, which I was certain wasn't something the SPVM would approve of.

Dee didn't approve of it either. They snatched Mitch's hat from his head before he could react.

"*Hey.*"

Dee held it away. "No. Listen, you can wear the hat, but this" —they pointed to the blue-and-gold shield on the front—"has to go." They turned and opened the top drawer of the makeup table and pulled out a roll of black tape. Muttering to themself, Dee started winding it around the cop hat to hide the blue band in addition to the shield. "Wasting my good tucking tape on this bullshit."

"That's going to come off, right?" Mitch asked, watching with a scowl on his face.

"Yes. Don't get your leather panties in a bunch, Mister Officer Sir. It's just micropore. I'll come right off your precious fascist symbol." Dee shoved Mitch's hat back in his hands.

Mitch's stared down at his masked hat, his nostrils flaring. His pecs seemed larger than usual, as did his biceps, and his abs a little more defined. Then I noticed his chest hair was damp with sweat—he'd probably done some push-ups and crunches to make himself look more muscular.

Jamming the hat back on his head, Mitch turned to me . . . and his expression softened.

"You look . . ."

I raised my brows. I hadn't even seen what Dee had done to my face yet. I turned to the mirror and stared at my reflection. The makeup wasn't outrageous or extravagant or even showy. It was . . . nice. My skin had a sheen to it and she had done something to my eyes that made them seem bigger, brighter. When I turned my head, my eyelids softly sparkled and, for once, my brows looked tidy. It wasn't feminine, but it wasn't masculine either. It was sort of . . . ethereal. I stood to see the whole effect with the sheer white bra and panties—suddenly, I wasn't embarrassed anymore.

"Huh," I said quietly.

"You like?" Dee grinned.

"Ye—"

"Yeah—" Mitch said, replying at the same time as me.

I laughed and turned back to him. "So, is this pretty enough?"

"It's fine," he replied gruffly, but there was a little pink in his cheeks. He glanced over at Dee. "Good job."

"Hang on. One . . . no, *two* more touches," they replied. They quickly dabbed some soft gloss to my lips, and then, after smoothing my hair into a wing to the side, they secured it in place with a little clip that had a bow made of white lace on it. "There. *Now* you're done." Then they looked over at Mitch. "Your turn."

"What? No." Mitch took a step back.

"Yes." Dee pointed to the chair. "Sit."

It looked like Mitch was going to refuse, but then, to my surprise, he balled his fists and sat down, staring at nothing.

Dee plucked the hat off his head and put it on his knee, then took out another little pallet of makeup and a small brush. In a few seconds, they had darkened the stubble on his upper lip so that it looked like he had a proper moustache, just like Tom of Finland's Kake.

"How's that?" Dee asked.

"Perfect." I grinned.

Mitch opened his eyes and looked in the mirror. His brows shot up, but he turned his head from side to side, appraising himself. He went to touch his face, but Dee swatted his hand away.

"Hang on. Close your eyes and hold your breath," Dee said, holding a small spray can in front of Mitch's face.

Mitch complied and Dee spritzed his face a few times.

"What was that?" Mitch asked with a grimace.

"Setting spray so you don't make a mess all over Patrick's face." Dee looked over at me with a coy glance and winked. "Or, do real men not kiss?"

Mitch just let out a low grunt and scowled, putting his hat back on, but when he turned to look at his reflection again, he looked pleased with himself. "Maybe I should grow one, eh?"

I didn't have a chance to reply because something started beeping, and Dee let out a string of curses.

"I have to go," they said, quickly draping a thin, silky green scarf around their neck and knotting it. "I have to present the next act, and I'm sitting here playing around with you two." They picked up some note cards from the table and shuffled through them. "Uh . . . you don't really have a chance for a drink. This next guy's a solo and he's only on for a ten-minute slot. A quick fap-and-go, as we call it. Then it's you. Um, you know the way to the stage?" Dee said to Mitch. "Well, there's a door on the left. Take that and it'll get you backstage. And then just come out when I announce you. Okay?" Dee then took off at a near sprint in their lofty platform heels, leaving Mitch and me alone in the dressing room.

This is really happening. I felt my heart knocking around in my ribcage, and a bead of nervous sweat trickled slowly down my back.

"What are we doing on stage?" I whispered, my mouth dry. "You'll tell me that, at least?"

Mitch looked down at me, his expression neutral. "What do you think? What we usually do, dipshit," he replied. But by now, I was certain he was reverting to being an asshole because he was just as nervous as I was.

Grasping his gloved hand, I took a deep breath and straightened my spine.

"All right. Let's go."

CHAPTER 19
HOLLOW AND TENDER

THE "FAP-AND-GO" was a *very* muscular Black man wearing only a
Batman cowl, a small cape, and tall black boots. Kneeling in the
centre of the stage, he was using a stroker emblazoned with the Bat-
Signal on the end and grunting rhythmically as he thrust his cock
into the toy. I grinned, glancing over at Mitch to see what he
thought of the show, but he was staring at the floor, seemingly lost
in thought as he pushed at an old piece of stage tape with the toe of
his boot. Next to Mitch, Dee was reading through their notecards,
occasionally shaking their head or sighing.

I turned back to watch the show just in time to see the man
quicken his strokes and then suddenly stop with a sharp exhale.

"I'm cumming," he said in a guttural, deadpan Batman voice. It
was weird and hilarious but also sorta hot. The man's chest heaved
and his thighs twitched for a moment, then he clenched his jaw
and slowly pulled the masturbator away. His long, cum-covered
dick slid out of the toy and swung a few times between his splayed
knees, dripping, then he climbed to his feet a little unsteadily.

The man bowed to scattered applause—there were only a dozen
or so people seated at the tables—then did a military-like swivel on

his heel and exited stage left. He paused to say something to Dee and then noticed me watching.

"What did you think of the show, pretty thing?" he asked, lifting the cowl off his sweat-streaked face, his voice softer now that he was no longer in character.

"It was funny and . . . sexy?" I replied honestly.

The man grinned. "Thanks."

Mitch grabbed my forearm and scowled as he pulled me away from the man. "Focus."

"Sorry."

Dee was out talking to the crowd as a couple of stagehands quickly mopped up the floor. A moment later, two more came out from the other side of the stage, carrying a bed between them. They placed it right in the centre of a big circle on the stage floor, then all four ran off stage.

"Next up we have some stage virgins . . ." Dee said into the mic, switching rapidly between French and English as they talked. I couldn't see their expression, but something made the audience laugh. " . . . and so, they've promised me that they're gonna put on quite a show for us tonight. However, they have requested that there be no direct audience participation."

Someone from the small crowd loudly said, "Aw!" and Dee chuckled. "I know! I know. However, you're welcome to join them on the stage for a closer look." Dee grinned and waggled their pointer finger back and forth. "But noooooo touching."

I let out a slow breath, relieved. My desire to get fucked by strangers had pretty much dried up, but while I would have submitted to it eagerly to make Mitch happy, I really didn't want a repeat of what had happened the last time he'd shared me.

"So put your hands together and welcome our newcomers to the stage: Officer Big Daddy and Pretty Boy."

Shit. I glanced over at Mitch and winced at the shock in his expression—obviously, Dee hadn't consulted him about the stage name.

"Mitch, I told Dee not to use the word dad—" I let out a yelp as Mitch clamped a hand on my shoulder, shoving me forward until I was on stage. The clapping grew louder with a few wolf whistles thrown in—I shielded my eyes from the bright lights and cast a glance at Dee who was smiling sweetly at Mitch, apparently immune to his murderous glare.

"Have fun, you two," Dee said, then blew a kiss and strutted off the stage.

Music began to play. It was nothing I recognized, but it had a nice beat. I looked at the crowd nervously, barely able to see anyone past the first row of tables. The dudes in jockstraps we had passed earlier were off to the left—one of them was getting a slow hand job from the man next to him, his eyes locked on me. At a table near the bar, there was an older woman in a fur coat with the collar pulled up to her ears, her features lit blue from below by the phone in her hand. At the nearest table sat a small group of shirtless young guys. All of them were toned and hairless, and one wore a crown and a sash that read "Bride" in flowing pink letters—they were talking above the music and judging by the dozens of empty shooter glasses in front of them, they'd been there a while.

"Take it all off!" someone shouted from beyond the spotlight's nimbus and I blushed. However, when I looked to Mitch for guidance, he seemed frozen in place, a trickle of sweat crawling from his temple to the corner of his jaw.

"Mitch?"

He turned slowly and I was stunned—he looked terrified. I quickly threw my arms around his neck, locking eyes with him, and that seemed to shake him out of it a bit, but I could see conflicting emotions in his darting gaze.

"We don't have to do this," I said quietly.

"The *fuck* we don't," Mitch muttered, though his voice lacked its usual bluff confidence. He swallowed and put his hands around my waist but didn't move them further. It was like he was completely paralyzed, and I think I knew why: he was about to divulge to everyone in the audience that he was, in fact, queer.

I went up on tip-toe and brought my lips close to his and murmured, "Mitch, you're about to fuck me in front of all these people. You're going to show them how your big, thick cock is the only one that gets to wreck my pussy. And then you're going to breed my hole because that's what it's there for . . ."

My words had the intended effect. I felt the tension drop out of his shoulders immediately, and he growled as he captured my mouth in a savage kiss. He grabbed my ass in both hands, lifting me up, so I wrapped my legs around his hips as we made out.

The crowd hooted and applauded, and I drew back for a second to grin at him.

"Show 'em you know how to fuck like a 'real man'," I said and bit my bottom lip coyly.

"Oh, shut the fuck up," Mitch replied, but his eyes crinkled at the corners as he gave me a quick smile. Then he attacked my mouth again and squeezed my ass cheeks, spreading them apart as he walked toward the front of the stage to show everyone that my hole was plugged. My dick pushed out the netting of the panties, and I was worried they would rip, but I had a feeling I wouldn't be wearing them for much longer.

Mitch set me down, turning me around to face the crowd while he grabbed a handful of hair to pull my head back, tugging on the butt plug at the same time until it held my hole open at the widest point. I whimpered, reaching up to clutch at his wrist so that he didn't rip my hair out, then gasped when he shoved the plug back in all the way. My cock ached but it didn't look like I was going to get any help there just yet. Mitch spun me around again and forced me down to my knees. I grasped the back of his thighs, staring up at him.

"Just unsnap it," he said loud enough for me to hear over the music.

It? I frowned, then looked at his leather pants, realizing that the front was a panel held in place by a series of black snaps running down from below his belt to between his legs. Curious, I grabbed both sides and tugged, and the whole panel came down, revealing his hardening cock.

I grinned up at Mitch. "Fancy."

"Keep going."

I was confused until I saw the panel went front to back and, when fully unsnapped, transformed Mitch's pants into what were essentially chaps. As if I couldn't get any harder—Mitch standing there with his thick cock jutting out of the black leather was *doing* things to me. . . I squeezed my dick through my panties and *moaned*.

Breathing hard, I dropped the leather panel on the ground and wrapped my hands around Mitch's shaft, opening my mouth wide to take him in. I heard murmurs from the audience and one "wow" as I started blowing him as best as I could without choking or gagging. It felt like I'd barely begun when he suddenly grabbed me by the hair again to haul me to my feet, bracing my lower back with his forearm so he could bend me backwards. Mitch bit *hard* into the side of my neck, causing me to let out a high-pitched squeal of pain, and pushed my bra up so he could tweak my nipple cruelly as he mauled me with his teeth.

Unable to stifle my shrieks of pain, I tearfully tried to push him away, but he held on, bending his knees to thrust his cock up between my thighs, rubbing its hot length against my balls and taint, adding his own precum to the mess already dripping down my inner thighs. With a deep, rumbling growl, Mitch abandoned my nipples to grab me by the back of my neck, his hand like a vise, and switched sides so he could savage the other side of my neck.

I was used to him manhandling me, but this was different. No longer in control of my body, I was just a doll in his arms, powerless to stop him from taking whatever he wanted from me. As I stood there trembling, my cheeks wet with tears . . . I felt myself slipping away . . .

Wait, no, *not* slipping away—opening up. As Mitch closed his teeth over my throat as if he meant to rip it out, I found myself craning my head further back, fingers hooked into his harness, pulling him into me, inviting his violence even though I sobbed out my breaths.

"*Fuck*, you're sexy," Mitch murmured against my jaw.

I cried out, a helpless sound, shivering as I soared so high I felt dizzy.

Mitch suddenly released me and I gasped, thinking I would drop to the floor, but he had moved us to the bed without me realizing it. I collapsed backwards on the mattress and then yelled out as he just yanked the plug from my ass, tearing the flimsy panties away in the process. Panting, he climbed on top of me, tossing his hat to the side before grabbing his thick cock in one gloved hand to point it at my throbbing pucker. Then, with a snarl, he shoved himself inside me to begin fucking me with a vengeance.

I yelled as my hole was forced open, my voice so hoarse it came out as a croak, and lay there helplessly as he hammered away at me. Then his thrusts began to slow, little by little, and he bent to find my mouth again, his tongue seeking mine out as his cock slid into me deep.

"Oh god," I whispered, pulling out of the kiss after only a few thrusts. "I'm going to cum."

"No, you're not."

My eyes popped open. "I'm not?"

"No." Mitch smiled at me as he continued fucking me slowly. "You're going to exert some fucking self-control and cum only when you're told to."

"Uh . . ." I licked my lips and squeezed my eyes shut, trying to ignore the thick cock moving inside me. "I . . . don't— Oh *fuck*." I panted, trying desperately to distract myself as he gave a sinister little chuckle.

Mitch suddenly pulled out and flipped me on my stomach to ram his cock back into me. Then, as soon as I was skirting the edge again, he lifted me to my knees and had me clutch the headboard, staring out at the crowd as he worked my hole. His fingers closed on my nipples, pinching them so hard that I let out a loud wail, my tears dripping from my chin to my chest while precum drooled from my cock.

The bridal party had quieted and sat staring in rapt silence as Mitch started growling in time to his thrusts. A man sitting at a table directly in front of me looked a little alarmed when Mitch wrapped his hands around my throat, cutting off my shrieks of pain, but he was obviously enjoying himself, given the fact that he was jerking off.

And he wasn't the only one.

Just as my vision began to swim, Mitch released me, and I drew in a ragged breath, eagerly pushing back into his battering cock; I was dangerously close to orgasm again, but I couldn't help myself. Then Mitch spun me around and I was on my back, my head hanging off the mattress, my legs up on Mitch's broad shoulders, bent over double as he continued to wreck my ass.

I began moaning louder—partially because of how good it felt, but mostly for the effect it was having on the audience—and Mitch laughed.

"Yeah, just like that. Show them how much you love taking dick, you slut." He curled his lip, thrusting faster, and I let out a shuddering breath, clutching the bedding as my pleasure quickly surged.

"Oh god." I swallowed, shaking my head as I fought for control. "If you don't want me to—*huhh huhh . . . fuck*—to cum, you . . ." I gritted my teeth, squeezing my eyes shut. "You should s-stop—"

Mitch did stop right then and pulled me off the bed, arranging me so that I was upside down, leaning back against the frame, resting on my shoulders and the back of my neck, my hands supporting my knees. Being in a piledriver position was always uncomfortable, but when Mitch turned around, facing away from me to push his cock down into my tender hole, I realized that no amount of discomfort was going to keep me from cumming at any moment. Panting, I watched Mitch's slick cock pistoning in my ass, then let out a reedy cry as I felt him swell inside me.

Mitch grunted, fucking me faster, then suddenly stilled. I could see the base of his dick jerk and his asshole throb as he bred my hole and I knew I had lost any hope of holding back my orgasm.

"*Now* it's your turn," Mitch said sounding breathless.

Oh thank fucking god. I tensed, teetering on the edge, then let out a strangled wail as the first pulse hit. My cum hit me in the face and, without even thinking, I grabbed my dick and aimed, opening my mouth to catch the next spurt as my hole convulsed around Mitch's cock. I squeezed my eyes closed as my climax raged through me, the spasms like waves rising from my core to crash through the throbbing cock in my fist.

Finally, I swallowed down my load, my balls hollow and tender, and just rested there, upside down and panting, grimacing as my hole clenched feebly at Mitch's dick a few last times.

"Holy *fuck*," I rasped, then giggled. My eyes popped open a second later when the audience broke into applause. I'd forgotten they were even there.

Mitch gently pulled out, and I slowly collapsed on my side on the cold floor, completely drained. When I eventually lifted my head, Mitch was gazing down at me with warmth in his pale blue eyes. He looked proud . . . proud and something else that woke the butterflies in my stomach.

"C'mere," he said softly and held out his hand.

I groggily climbed to my feet with his help, then gasped when he took me up in his arms. I laid my head on his shoulder, nuzzling into the crook of his neck as he carried me offstage.

"You did good, kid," he said, his quiet voice rumbling against my ear. "Really good."

. . .

The panties had been destroyed during the show and I'd ditched the bra, not bothering to put on anything to cover up my nakedness as I sat next to Mitch, sipping at my vodka cranberry. Dee was on stage singing a medley of pop songs from the eighties while doing a little burlesque-type striptease routine. They had a great singing voice and the dance was a lot of fun to watch—I was glad we'd stayed. I turned to Mitch to say just that and saw that his gaze was on me and not the stage. He was watching me with a little wrinkle between his brows.

"What?" I asked, giving him a crooked smile.

Mitch just lifted a shoulder and shook his head, his frown deepening for a moment, then he sighed. "Nothing."

"Huh," I replied, cocking my head at him. "You all right?"

He didn't reply; he just kept staring into my eyes, making my ribcage ache . . . like it was suddenly too small to contain my heart.

I stood and leaned over him to kiss him softly, tasting whisky on his lips as I reached down to unsnap his pants. Then, without a word, I turned around to ease myself down on Mitch's quickly stiffening cock, the lube in my well-bred hole making it effortless to take him to the hilt. Mitch groaned and wrapped his arms around me, holding me tight as he pressed his lips to the side of my neck.

"Mmm," he said quietly, then gave another long, trembling sigh.

I ran my fingers along Mitch's forearm and was rewarded with another happy rumble. Smiling, I leaned back in his embrace, watching Dee's performance with Mitch's thick cock deep inside me where it belonged.

CHAPTER 20
REMINDERS

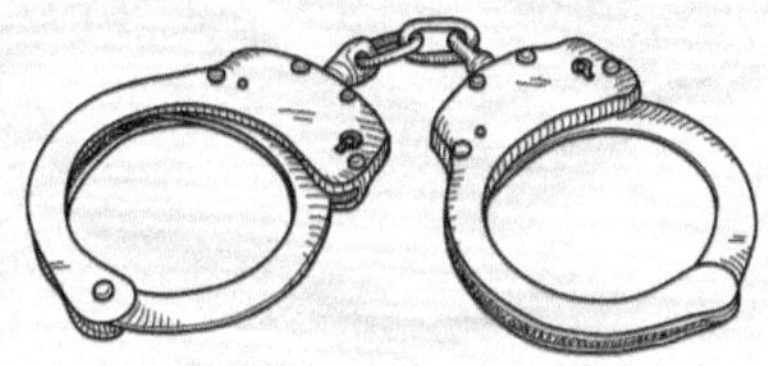

JULY

"Do you have any cash?" I called out to Mitch.

"Depends. Why do you need it?" he replied, frowning as he poked his head out of the bathroom. He had streaks of shaving cream on his square jaw.

"Laundry tokens," I replied.

"All right. Check my wallet. There should be a fiver in there." Mitch ducked back into the bathroom.

I went to the coffee table and picked up Mitch's leather wallet. The exterior was worn through in places, and when I opened it, it was so weathered it felt like all it would take was a little tug and I could rip it in two. I smiled, mentally filing "new wallet" under possible birthday gifts for Mitch next month. After finding a crisp blue five-dollar bill inside the fold, something in the card slots caught my eye. Sliding it out, I frowned—it was my old Concordia University ID. *Huh.* I thought I had thrown it out. I wrinkled my nose at the picture. It was faded, but you could still see that my complexion was horrible and that my barber had done me dirty and cut off *way* too much. *Why does he have this?*

"What are you doing?"

I straightened, fumbling with the card and wallet as Mitch glared at me. "I was just . . . uh . . ." I tried to get my ID to fit into the little leather sleeve, but it wouldn't go in. "I just—"

"*Jesus*. Gimme that," Mitch replied, plucking the wallet out of my hands. His brows pinched together over his nose as he stared at my old ID, then his jaw clenched as he jammed the card back in place.

He was *blushing*.

I blinked—was he doing the equivalent of carrying a picture of me in his wallet? *Oh my god.*

"So, uh, why do you have my old card with you?" I asked with a coy smile.

Instead of replying, Mitch tucked his wallet into his back pocket and looked around impatiently.

"Where's my fucking coffee?"

"Oh. Right. Sorry," I replied and ran into the kitchen where I had put his coffee in a travel mug. "Here."

Mitch accepted the mug with a nod, then furrowed his brow.

"Aren't you going to be late?" he asked.

"Nah, I got plenty of time," I replied. "I'm going to start a load of laundry first, and then I'll head out. Aren't *you* going to be late?"

Mitch curled his lip. "Don't be a smartass."

I smiled, then went up on tiptoe to give him a brief kiss. "I'll see you after your shift."

"Hm," he grunted, then pressed his thumb to my bottom lip gently before turning to set his mug down on the table to continue getting suited up for work.

I slung my laptop bag over my shoulder and picked up my coffee.

"Bye," I said, opening the front door. I kicked the laundry bag out the door onto the front steps. "Try not to shoot anyone today!" I slammed the door shut before he could reply and chuckled to myself as I picked up the bag of laundry. Maybe that bit of sass would earn me a spanking later . . . I *hoped* so.

I went around the side of our duplex to the basement where the machines were. After I got the laundry going with some fresh tokens, I locked back up, and started down the sidewalk, humming to myself. It was warm out but not muggy and it was supposed to be sunny and breezy all day—*exactly* the sort of weather that used to inspire me to find rando dick in the park once the sun went down. But those days were behind me and I didn't miss it a bit.

Don't you, though? Just a little? I stifled the thought with a scowl.

"Wow, *you* look like you're in a mood."

Startled, I stopped walking and turned to look at the man I had just passed. He was a little taller than I was, with a reddish beard and moustache, and was wearing a plaid Peaky Blinders-type cap, a ratty Regina Spektor T-shirt, and some oversized cargo shorts. He was watching me with obvious amusement.

"Um. Are you talking to me?" I asked.

"I wasn't talking to the squirrels, *darling*." The man chuckled. "What's giving you the stink-eye? Did your mean ol' daddy do something to you, Patrick?"

I gaped at him in total confusion for a few seconds before my brain finally caught on. It was like one of those optical illusion posters where the image suddenly comes out if you stare at it the right way.

"Oh my god, *Dee*? I didn't recognize you." I remembered their preference for he/they when they weren't in makeup, and this masculine version of the person I knew was definitely not wearing any. He was reasonably good-looking but in a very plain, unassuming sort of way—completely the opposite of Dee.

"Bruno," he replied with a grin.

"*Bruno*?" I laughed. "Okay. I wouldn't have guessed that was your real name in a million years."

"Blame my mother," Bruno said, wrinkling his nose. "So, hey, where've you been? We were hoping for another little show with you two, but you've been a no-show. What's up with that?"

Mitch and I had performed three times at the Péché Sacré but it had been weeks since we'd even talked about doing it again.

"I guess we just got busy?"

"Busy and getting *fit*," Bruno replied, reaching out to squeeze my shoulder. "You're looking good, kid."

I felt heat in my cheeks. "Thanks. I go to the gym with Mitch four times a week."

"He's not trying to turn you into a hardbody like him, is he?" Bruno's brows rose.

"Nah. Just . . . toning. And stuff." I shifted my laptop bag so the strap wasn't digging into my neck anymore. "And uh, I've been really busy with school."

"School?"

"Yeah, McGill started up a new business program for the game development sector. I got in for the summer semester—the courses are intensive and they're kicking my ass, but I think I'm doing okay."

"That's *fantastic*!" Bruno exclaimed. "I guess your fans'll just have to wait until you have time for them, Mister Academic." His voice shifted to the register he used when he was Dee. "Look at me *beaming* over here like someone's mum. I'm so proud!"

"Thanks," I said with a chuckle. "So, what are you doing in my end of NDG? Didn't you say you lived near Girouard?"

"I do . . . but I'm meeting an old friend for coffee," Bruno said, then reached out to touch my shoulder again. "Hey, we two should go for a coffee and gab, eh?"

"Patrick, what the *fuck* are you doing?"

Bruno snatched his hand back like he had touched a hot burner and turned to Mitch who had pulled up next to us in his cruiser. "Oh hel—"

"Take a walk, asshole," Mitch said with a growl in his voice as he leaned out the window.

"Mitch it's okay, it's ju—" I tried.

"Shut your hole, Patrick. I'm talking to the jackoff in the stupid hat." Mitch opened the door and stepped out, glaring down at Bruno. "You deaf or just stupid? I said beat it."

"Well, *Christ*." Bruno crossed his arms, shaking his head as he stared up at Mitch. "Honey, as far as I'm concerned, *you're* the asshole in the stupid hat. Lordy, I don't know what dear Patrick sees in your boorish, moronic, mouthbreathing . . . *nonsense*." Bruno gestured to Mitch from head to toe, then tilted his head sassily as a vein rose up in Mitch's forehead. "What? You gonna bash my brains in with your little club and smear my queer ass all over the sidewalk, you fucking fascist neanderthal?"

Terrified, I stood frozen in place, worried that Mitch would do exactly that, but then Mitch's brow wrinkled up.

"Dee?" he asked, his voice faint.

"It's Bruno. Nice to see you too, *pig*."

I clapped my hand over my mouth before the laugh escaped as I watched Mitch's face contort. But it seemed he wouldn't hurt Bruno . . . I'd seen Dee put Mitch in his place or insult him at least a dozen times now and no matter what, Mitch always backed down. I wondered why that was. Did Dee/Bruno have something on him, or was it just a weird sort of . . . respect?

Mitch cleared his throat. "Didn't recognize you there."

"I get that a lot," Bruno replied drily.

"All right, uh . . . Patrick. Get your ass to school," Mitch said awkwardly as he got back into the cop car.

"What? No kiss goodbye for your dear sweet boy?" Bruno narrowed his eyes, his grin taunting. "*Tsk*. You're still too afraid the straights'll see you and realize you're a big ol' homo, aren't you?"

Mitch frowned and shut the car door, then shot me a quick self-conscious glance before speeding away.

Bruno laughed. "I don't get it. And I don't think I will *ever* get what you see in that man . . . except maybe that fat cock he has. But"—he turned back to me with a crooked smile—"you do you, baby. 'Cause it's obviously doing *something* for the two of yous." Bruno shook his head. "Honestly, though, I don't see it lasting . . . if you want to hear my bitchy opinion."

"It'll be a year . . . next week," I said quietly, just realizing it then. *Huh.*

"Is that so?" Bruno tilted his head again, appraising me with a strange expression. I always wondered if he knew something about how Mitch and I had started off. Had Mitch told him? "Well. *Mazel tov*, I guess. Oh shit!" Bruno suddenly leaned towards me and gave me quick cheek *bisous*. "I really gotta be off, honey. But we should do that coffee! I'll be in touch."

"Okay," I replied, and watched Bruno's back as he walked quickly away to meet with his friend.

A whole *year* since Mitch had stepped into my life. Was I *really* going with that first encounter as the start of our . . . relationship? I shook my head and turned back toward the metro station, hoping I wouldn't be late for class.

Since I couldn't pinpoint the day when things changed between Mitch and me, I guess I was stuck with that date. I let out a slow breath through my nose as my Chucks pounded the sidewalk, hoping to catch the bus at the station before it left.

Our anniversary would be a toxic reminder, year after year, wouldn't it?

CHAPTER 21
THE CALL

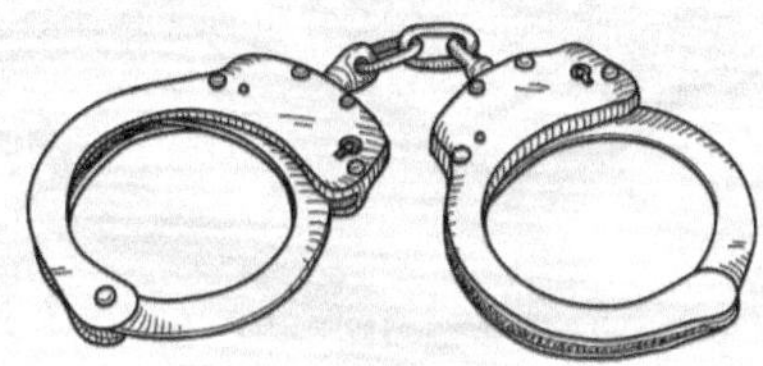

I woke up to an empty bed and glanced at the clock. It was just past one. Mitch should have been home by now.

I sat up, an uneasy feeling in my stomach, and reached for my phone. Had Bruno spooked Mitch earlier that day? Was Mitch out getting drunk because of it? He hadn't done that in months . . .

"Shit," I muttered when my phone wouldn't respond, then noticed I hadn't plugged it in properly—the cable was plugged into the space between the case and the phone and not in the actual charging socket—and the battery had drained. I plugged my phone in the right way and turned it on. I hoped I hadn't missed too many messages from Mitch.

Or maybe he didn't leave you any messages at all. Maybe he went out to a bar and picked someone up and is fucking them right now.

"Ugh, shut up, dipshit," I whispered to my brain.

Finally, the screen brightened and I thumbed in my code.

Three text messages. The first was from Uber Eats about a special.

The next two were from Mitch. They had come in ten minutes apart, just after eleven:

Be home soon.

A domestic. Running late.

A domestic? Did he mean a domestic disturbance call? Why hadn't he updated me since then? Worried, I typed and sent:

Where are you?

I waited for him to reply but then noticed there was a new voicemail. Frowning, I tapped the button and lifted the phone to my ear. I felt my heart drop into my stomach as I listened to the woman's message.

Mitch.

An incident.

A hospital address.

Oh god.

CHAPTER 22

LIFE AND DEATH

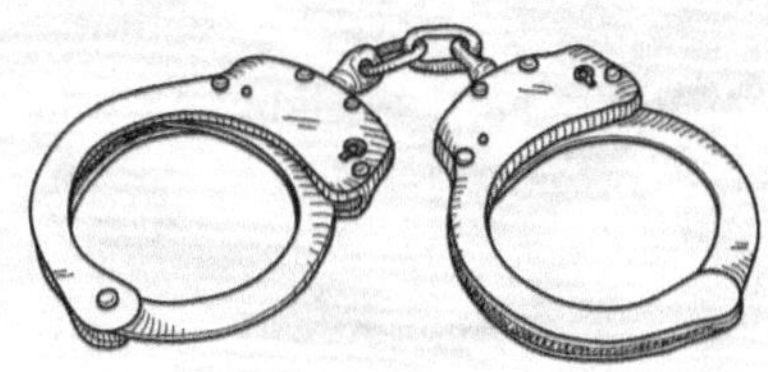

I shifted from foot to foot as I stared at the man in front of me. It had taken me less than twenty minutes by Uber to get to the hospital, only to be met by a long line of people waiting to speak to the woman at the desk. I tapped my foot, sighing, then looked at my phone, wishing I'd had time to charge it for more than just a few minutes. The battery was at two percent. No, *one* percent.

An incident? What kind of incident? Did he get stabbed? Was he shot? Or . . . did his crazy driving finally land him in the hospital? I chewed my thumbnail and wrapped my other arm around my midsection tight, like I could somehow shrink the anxiety building inside me by holding it in.

Oh no. What if it's his heart? What if he's got what his father had?

Fuck fuck fuck fuck. At the front of the line, a woman was explaining something in halting French while pointing to the crumpled documents she had dug out of her bag. *Fuck fuck fuck . . . Mitch you better be all right, you asshole.*

Hospital staff pushing a woman on a gurney raced by and slammed through a pair of swinging doors, startling me, and I caught a glimpse of the Emergency Room on the other side. The woman who left the voicemail had said Mitch was in the ER, but not *where* in the ER. Were there ER rooms or was it just the big, bustling room beyond with all the blue curtains that I had just seen?

Fuck fuck fuck fuck . . . fuck *it.* Taking a deep breath, I stepped out of the queue at triage and ran for the doors, throwing them open as someone yelled, "*Monsieur! Monsieur!*" behind me. I scanned the row of hospital beds to my left and right as I walked, then doubled back to check behind a few curtains. The doctors and nurses, who had largely ignored me thus far, did *not* like that at all—I was quickly apprehended by a very tall orderly in purple scrubs.

"Please," I said, struggling. Tears ran down my cheeks and my nose dripped. "I need to see Mitch. Mitch McKenzie. Michel? Michel McKenzie? *Tu le connais? Y-est où?* I need to see him."

"Whoa, whoa," the man holding me said in a gentle voice. "Just relax, dude."

I stopped trying to wiggle out of his grasp and just stood there panting. "I'm sorry. I just need to see—"

"Patrick?" The weak voice came from behind the curtain to my right and I ducked under the orderly's arm, breaking his grasp on my shoulder in the process. I grabbed the blue curtain and tugged it aside. Mitch looked so pale and sickly, lying there with tubes coming from his nose and his arms and his chest. It was like he had shrunk—he seemed half his size.

"Oh my god, Mitch," I cried, grabbing the side of his bed. "Oh my god."

"I'm sorry, but you can't be in here," the nurse said in French, turning around. He held up a hand. "It's family *only*. Are you family?"

"I'm . . ." I stood there in a daze, trying to come up with an answer. "I'm . . . uh . . ."

"He's my fiancé." Mitch's brow furrowed with the effort of lifting a hand to clasp mine weakly. His skin was clammy.

"All right," the nurse replied, not seeming convinced but

obviously willing to look the other way. "I'll be right back with the doctor to explain the situation."

"Thank you," I whispered, squeezing Mitch's hand. "Thank you."

The man left and Mitch frowned at me. "Took you fucking long enough," he said, his voice low. He winced as he shifted, then inhaled quickly—he was obviously in pain.

"My phone . . . the . . . I was sleeping . . . and my phone. The, uh, plug . . ." I replied, gesturing vaguely. I hiccupped a sob and stopped trying to explain. I went down on one knee next to the bed, clutching onto his hand. "What *happened?*"

"Jesus. Will you stop it?" Mitch curled his lip in disgust, then suddenly coughed into his fist. "*Fuck.*"

"Tell me what happened—did you get shot?"

"Ha." He closed his eyes and shook his head. "No. I was impaled."

"*Impaled?*" I stared in horror. "Like, stabbed?"

A deep wrinkle formed between Mitch's brow, then he opened his eyes. They were bloodshot. "No. Nothing like that." He shifted in place again, sighing. "Tank and I answered a call. Some shithead was beating his wife. We get there and the two of them are high as balls, whaling on each other out front of their apartment building." Mitch coughed and grimaced. "So I go to step between them, like to break it up, and the fucker just pushes me. Lost my balance. Fell back. Landed on one of those goddamn metal fences they put around gardens, you know? One of the pointy bits popped right through my vest at the back." He closed his eyes again, breathing heavily.

"And he's lucky that it wasn't an inch to the left, or else he wouldn't be here right now."

I looked over to see a short Asian woman wearing pale green scrubs and a blue surgical mask. Her glasses had small silver stars on the rims.

Her eyes smiled gently at me. "I'm Doctor Phan. I'm really glad you made it in time."

"In . . . time?" Eyes wide, I stared at her. "In time for his surgery?"

"Oh." The doctor's gaze went to Mitch. "Well, I'm afraid it's too late for that."

"Too late?" I wrenched myself to my feet, reeling in shock. "What do you mean too *late*?"

"What the doc means is I'm dying, Patrick," Mitch replied with a strange little smile.

I yanked my hand out of his, angry. "Stop it. It's not *funny*. Ha ha." I wiped my face and crossed my arms. "Stop the bullshit."

"The finial punctured his liver," Dr. Phan said quietly. "He suffered a hepatic artery avulsion and, while we were able to stop the bleeding, the liver won't survive the damage."

Blinking at her rapidly, I tried to make sense of what she was saying.

"She means the fence nicked something important, so my liver's caput."

I turned to Mitch, barely able to see him through the tears in my eyes. "You're *really* dying?"

"Seem like it." Mitch exhaled hard and clenched his jaw. "Sucks to be me."

"And there's nothing they can do?" I asked in a small voice.

"I'm afraid short of a transplant . . . " Dr. Phan shook her head. "And there's very little chance we'd get a liver in time. He's got hours, not days."

"Oh my god," I said, feeling like my legs would give out. "Oh god no."

"Hey, it's *okay*, Patrick. It's fine. I had a good run, you know?"

I scowled at him, my chest heaving. "No. No, it's *not* okay. I don't want you to die. You *can't* die." Then I gasped, turning to the doctor. "Wait. Wait a sec. A transplant. Can you do a transplant from a live person? Like, someone can give him half their liver? I think I saw that on an episode of House. Is that a real thing?"

A ridge of thin wrinkles appeared on the doctor's forehead. "Well, *yes*. Of course. But the donor would have to be a match, and—"

"I'll do it," I said, reaching for Mitch's hand again. "I'll give him half my liver."

"What?" Mitch's eyes went wide.

"I'm a universal donor. O negative. And, and, and . . . I don't drink much. I'm healthy. I have no diseases or anything. Yes. Let's do this," I said, excitement making my words run together.

"Are you certain? We'll have to run a few quick tests, and we don't have a lot of time," Dr. Phan said, but her tone matched my enthusiasm.

"Can we have a moment, doctor?" Mitch said, his voice quiet and steady.

"Yes. But just a few minutes. I'm going to start getting the ball rolling," Dr. Phan replied briskly, ducking out of the curtained ER bay.

"Patrick. No," was all that Mitch said as he gazed up at me.

"I'm doing it."

"No. You're not. It's insanity. Why the hell would you put yourself in harm's way like this? I refuse."

I whimpered, holding his hand in both of mine. "Please. Please, you can't die. You *can't*."

Mitch scrutinized my face for a few long seconds. "I'm not a good man, Patrick. I did bad things to you."

"Doesn't matter. I won't let you die. I *need* you."

A wry smirk dimpled Mitch's cheeks. His skin had an unhealthy yellow cast to it. "You need me, huh?"

"I do." My bottom lip trembled as I held his gaze. "More than anything."

Mitch heaved a slow sigh, then coughed into his fist again. "If I let you do this. *If*—" His face contorted in pain again for a moment . . . or was he fighting back tears? "God*damn* it. *If* I let you do this, you have to realize it changes *nothing* between us. I'm not suddenly gonna bend over backwards for your sorry ass just because you're too dumb to realize you'd be better off without me."

I sagged, feeling dizzy with relief. He was going to let me save his life. I just stood there for a moment, soaring on endorphins; then I forced myself to give him a mischievous grin, even though tears still ran freely down my face.

"What about the fact that I'm supposedly your *fiancé* now? That's a pretty big change, I'd say."

"Oh, for fucks' sake. I just said that so they'd let you in."

"So we're not getting married then?" I brought his hand up to my lips so I could kiss his knuckles. "Why didn't you go with 'boyfriend'?"

"Because we're not in fucking high school, dipshit. And boyfriends aren't family."

"Partner?" I said, letting my smile widen.

"You're neither a cop and we don't play tennis." He smiled.

I rested my cheek against the back of his hand, my pulse ticking up again, realizing I was about to go into major surgery.

"Hey, Mitch?"

"What?"

"Can I ask you to do one thing in return?"

"Jesus," Mitch said, then started muttering like he was talking to himself. "First he talks me into something I didn't even want, and now he's making demands." He scowled at me. "What is it?"

"I don't want you to be a cop anymore."

It was like Mitch had frozen in place, not breathing or even blinking.

"It's not like you *have* to work right now anyway, not with the house getting sold for so much. You could find something else to do. Maybe start your own company or something," I said, desperately hoping I hadn't just ruined everything. "I just . . . I just don't want to be with a cop. I hate cops . . . and I hate that part of you. For *many* reasons."

Mitch's eyes narrowed as he lay there in silence

"Please? It's not that big an ask, *is* it?" I murmured.

Finally, Mitch replied. "Well . . . I guess not," he said in a hoarse voice. "If it makes you happy . . ." Mitch closed his eyes with a sigh. "All right . . . *fuck*. I was getting too old for that bullshit anyway, right?"

I let out a small cry and threw myself down to hug him.

"Hey! Ow. Ow . . . *shit*. Careful, dumbass. Are you *trying* to kill me now?" Mitch shoved at me unconvincingly. "I thought you were trying to save my ass." He chuckled, then sucked in a breath through clenched teeth.

"Sorry," I said, straightening.

Someone cleared their throat and I turned, startled.

"We should really get things started," said Dr. Phan. "That is, if you're a hundred percent certain you want to go through with this."

"I am," I said, smiling down at Mitch. Were his eyes a little wet, or was it the light? "A hundred percent."

The first thing I became aware of was the nausea. It seeped into the dark, rousing me from my sleep. I opened my eyes, feeling like I was on a rocking ship, and realized I was in a hospital bed. *Right. The operation.* I blinked groggily at the saline bag hanging next to me and grimaced, my stomach roiling.

"Oh, there you are," said a woman's voice in French. She peered down at me over her surgical mask. Her eyes were bright green with a fleck of golden brown in the right iris. "How are you feeling? Nauseous?"

I nodded and she pulled a narrow syringe out from somewhere, plunging it into the tube that snaked down to my hand.

"There. That should make you feel better in no time."

"Where . . .?"

"You're in Recovery. We'll have you in your room in a bit, don't worry."

"Surgery?" I asked, my voice barely audible. "Went well?"

Her eyes narrowed for a moment. "Just rest. All right?"

Darkness swallowed me up before I could reply.

When I woke again, I was in a hospital room. The saline bag was still there and I had a plastic thingy on my finger. It was dark outside . . . night. What night? How long had I been there?

I grimaced and started to sit up but gave up almost immediately. I was in pain and felt *so* weak and tired. I lifted the thin blanket and saw the bandage on my abdomen. It was smaller than I'd assumed. Obviously, it had gone well for me, but . . . I glanced around, discovering I was alone.

Where is Mitch?

My heart stilled in my chest. What if we were too late? What if he didn't make it?

"Hello?" I rasped. "Is there anyone there?" In a panic, I ran my hands along the sides of the hospital bed, looking for a button or a switch or *something* to summon *someone*. "Hello?"

A moment later, the door opened, letting in bright light from the hallway.

"Did he make it?" I asked the silhouette in the doorway. "Is he okay?"

"Uh . . . one moment, I will get someone," he replied. The way the nurse or orderly quickly retreated did nothing to quell my fears.

I waited in agony for someone to come tell me whether Mitch was alive or dead. Finally, the door creaked open again.

"Do you mind if I turn a few lights on?" the man asked.

"No, that's fine." I cleared my voice. "So, is he okay?"

The man turned the light on in the bathroom and then clicked on a small light next to my bed, making the room a little brighter but not so bright that it hurt my eyes.

"I'm Doctor Mbaye," the man said in Senegalese-accented French, coming to stand at my bedside. He wore an orange surgical cap and royal blue scrubs with a paper surgical mask dangling from one ear. He stared down at me solemnly, clasping his hands one over the other in front of him, holding a folder. "I am afraid there were some complications with the surgery. Your father suffered a heart attack while he wa—"

"He's not my father," I blurted out automatically.

"Oh?" Dr. Mbaye's eyes widened, and then his face creased in an apologetic grimace. "I'm sorry. I just assumed."

The doctor's words suddenly hit me like a brick to the face. *Heart attack?*

"Oh my god, Mitch is *dead?*" I did manage to sit up this time despite the pain. I let out a ragged breath, my heart collapsing on itself as the ground opened up beneath me.

"No! No, no . . ." the doctor said, shaking his head rapidly. "No. It was a *minor* infarction. But, that's how we discovered he had a congenital heart defect and were subsequently able to repair it. It just meant he was in surgery longer than you. He is resting now and should make a full recovery. I don't think I've ever said this before, but it was a *good* thing he had a heart attack on our table. We would have never known about the defect and he would have almost certainly suffered a fatal myocardial infarction in the future. . ."

As the doctor explained, my mind was reeling. *Mitch was alive.* Not only was he alive, but he wouldn't have to worry about dying the same way his dad or uncle had.

"When can I see him?" I asked impatiently, interrupting Dr. Mbaye.

The doctor chuckled. "I was *about* to say that we will bring him to you shortly. Now lie back down before you pop a staple and ruin my nice clean work." He helped me settle back into bed properly. "Now, don't worry, Patrick. All will be well. Your friend is strong."

"Yeah," I whispered, nodding quickly as I clutched at the blanket. "Okay. Thank you."

Dr. Mbaye patted my hand. "You're welcome."

It felt like an eternity before the door opened again. This time, it was a group of five orderlies surrounding a gurney. They quickly wheeled the bed into the spot next to mine and got busy setting up various pieces of equipment, but the only thing I had eyes for was Mitch's tired but smiling face. Finally, the flurry of activity ended, and after they made sure that Mitch was comfortable, they left us alone.

"How's it going," I said, feigning nonchalance when all I wanted to do was climb into his hospital bed.

Mitch snorted. "Peachy. You?"

"I'm better . . . *now*."

"Oh good lord," he replied, pulling a face. "You're not going to be a fucking sap about this, are you?"

I grinned. "Sorry."

He let out a soft grunt. "You know . . . for the record, I still think you hate yourself."

"How's that?" I asked with a frown.

"Because you were willing to do this to yourself just to be with an asshole like me."

I smirked. "Ah. But you see, now I get to tell people that you *love* it when I'm inside you."

"Oh *god*." Mitch's expression twisted, and then he quickly pinched the bridge of his nose, the muscles rolling in his jaw.

Alarmed, I rose up on my elbow, wondering if I had gone too far with my stupid joke.

"Mitch?"

Mitch let out a low wheeze, his eyes squeezed tight.

"Hey . . . hey, Mitch?"

"Jesus fucking Christ, Patrick . . . I've just had heart surgery and a liver transplant. Now is *not* the time to make me laugh, dipshit."

"Sorry," I replied, holding back my own laughter for fear of hurting myself. "I couldn't help it." I settled back down and sighed when Mitch's gaze met mine again. I stretched out my hand as far as I could, and, after a pause, he did the same. Only our fingers could touch, but it was enough.

"For the record, you *are* an asshole," I said.

"Yeah. I know."

"Like, would it kill you to say 'thank you'?"

"Oh *fuck* off," Mitch growled . . . then he smiled and what I saw in his eyes was worth so much more than a simple thank you.

It meant everything.

EPILOGUE

15 YEARS LATER

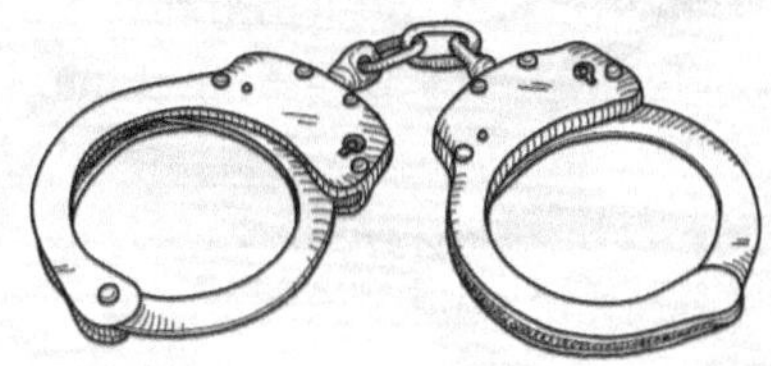

JULY

"So, you met Uncle Patrick in a *park*?" asked Mya, folding her little hands under her chin as she looked from Mitch to me. "What were you doing in a park? Did you push him on a swing?"

"Not a park with swings, kiddo. A big green park with lots and lots of trees. And . . . uh, benches." Mitch winked at me and I shook my head with a smile. *Asshole.*

"Oh," said Kenny. "That sounds like a boring park. What's the point?"

"Are you pestering your uncles?" asked Jenny, picking up the dirty dishes from the picnic table. She'd lost too much weight since Laurent had passed away in the fall—her wedding ring slid to her knuckle as she reached for a balled-up napkin.

"I just was cu-ree-ous, Nana," Mya said. "Uncle Mitch says he met Uncle Patrick in a park with no swings."

"Is that so?" Jenny said, grinning.

"That is a fact," I replied.

"And then what happened?" Kenny asked.

"Well . . ." Mitch took a sip of beer, turning to smile at me. "I saw the handsomest young man I had ever seen, and I decided right then and there that I would do everything in my power to make him like me."

Jenny straightened, a skeptical look on her face. "*Really?* You? Try to make someone like you?" She snorted.

Mitch shrugged and grinned, taking another swig. His hair had gone a bright steel grey, but he still had most of it, and though his face was lined, he didn't look his age. If anything, I thought he was even more handsome than when we had met. I didn't think time had been as kind to me, but I never saw that when he looked at me. I smiled and reached for his hand, squeezing it.

"If that's how he wants to sell it . . ." I said with a shrug. It wasn't the truth of how we started out, but it wasn't a lie either. I could see the kids were getting bored with our cryptic conversation, so I reached over and opened my bag. "So, who wants to try a brand-new game?"

"Me!" Kenny's hand shot up and his sister climbed to her feet on the picnic bench, hopping up and down.

"Me me me me me!" Mya yelled with both hands in the air.

I laughed and pulled out *Chipmunk Mansion* and held it up.

"Hang on," Jenny said, snatching it out of my hand. "Rémi said the last game you brought them gave them nightmares. He and Nico made me promise they wouldn't get any more scary games from Uncle Patrick." She peered at the back of the box.

"Yeah, I'm sorry about that. I really didn't think that the little skeleton guy in *Flower Ashes* could be so scary to kids . . . but it was *really* good feedback for our developers. We changed things up and bumped the rating and so far, so good," I said. "I promise . . . the scariest thing with *Chipmunk Mansion* is the pile of dirty dishes in the kitchen. I swear."

"All right, you two," Jenny said, handing over the box to her squealing grandkids. "Let's go get this set up in the living room VR unit, shall we? *But* . . . we'll wash our hands first, right?"

"Right, Nana," the two replied dutifully.

I watched the trio retreat into the big converted farmhouse and took Mitch's hand again.

"You know, you still haven't apologized for what you did to me back then," I said, bringing his knuckles to my lips.

Mitch's mouth turned down at the corners. "Meh."

"Meh?"

"What? You *want* me to fucking apologize?" Mitch said, narrowing his eyes.

"Well . . . it *would* be nice . . ." I said, lifting my brows as I smiled sweetly at him.

"You know what *would* be nice, dipshit?"

"What would be nice, sweetheart?" I replied, reaching under the table with my free hand to squeeze his cock through his pants.

"Mmm." Mitch closed his eyes, and then he chuckled. "I was going to say it would be nice if you shut your goddamn mouth . . . but now I think I'd prefer your mouth open."

"Oh yeah?" I leaned in to kiss the side of his neck while I fondled him.

"Yeah. *Wide* open."

"Uh huh?" I murmured against his warm skin. Despite having already fucked that morning, he was quickly stiffening in my grip. Age had done nothing to slow him down in that regard.

Mitch turned his head and caught my mouth in a brief kiss, then pulled away, his eyes crinkling at the corners.

"Keep that up, and I'll be forced to wreck your cunt," he said quietly.

"Oh?" I tilted my head at him as I quickly tugged down his zipper and slipped my hand into the opening. "Is that a promise?"

Mitch's eyes closed again with his soft groan as I played with his cock. He swallowed audibly, then focused on me again, a deep wrinkle between his brows as he curled his lip.

"What do *you* think, dumbass?"

I grinned.

LEXICON

OF MONTREAL/QUEBEC/CANADIAN OR
FRENCH-LANGUAGE TERMS

BIXI - BIXI Montréal is a public bicycle-sharing system serving Montreal. (Montreal)

Bonne Chance - Good Luck

Chu dans marde - Literally, I'm in shit aka I'm in trouble. (Quebec)

Depanneur (often shortened to dep) - A convenience/corner store or bodega. (Quebec)

Laval - An island to the north-west of Montreal, across Rivière des Prairies (Prairies River). (Quebec)

Loonie - The Canadian one-dollar coin, named as such because of the common loon on one side of many of them (there are other versions). (Canada)

May two-four - The Victoria Day long weekend is often called "May two-four" for two reasons: Victoria Day falls on May 24, and two-four is slang for a case of twenty-four beers, which is definitely enjoyed over the long weekend. (Canada)

Médecins Sans Frontièrs - Doctors Without Borders.

Montreal (Mohawk: *Tiohtià:ke)* - Montreal is a city in Quebec, Canada. Most of it is on the island of Montreal, but there is suburban sprawl beyond. Montreal is the 10th largest city in North America and is one of the most bilingual cities in Quebec *and* Canada, with almost 60% of the population able to speak both English and French.

NDG - Notre-Dame-de-Grâce (sometimes affectionately called The Deeg) is a neighbourhood (*my* neighbourhood, actually) located in the Côte-des-Neiges–Notre-Dame-de-Grâce residential borough of Montreal. (Montreal)

SPVM - *Service de Police de la Ville de Montréal* aka the Montreal police force. (Montreal)

The Village - The Gay Village in Montreal. It is the largest gay village in North America in terms of area. (Montreal)

Ville-Émard - A neighbourhood located in the Sud-Ouest borough of Montreal. (Montreal)

West Island - The western part of Montreal Island. Largely Anglophone. (Montreal)

BOOKS BY BEY DECKARD

Uncle Zach

Better the Devil You Know

Exposed

Beauty and His Beast

The Blacksmith's Apprentice

SHORT STORIES

Don't Touch Me (UnCommon Bodies Anthology)

Rakka Surprise (UnCommon Lands Anthology)

ABOUT THE AUTHOR

Artist, Writer, Dog Lover

Bey Deckard is the author of a bunch of novels including the *Baal's Heart books, Max, Beauty and His Beast,* and *Better the Devil You Know.*

Bey lives in Montréal, Canada where he spends most of his time writing, doing graphic work, painting portraits, speaking French, cooking tasty vegetarian eats, or watching more movies than is good for him. If you're the curious type, www.beydeckard.com is where you'll find art and free stories by Bey as well as information on his published works.

bey.deckard@gmail.com
Look for Deckard's Diablerie on Facebook

facebook.com/authorbeydeckard

x.com/BeyDeckard

instagram.com/beydeckard

goodreads.com/beydeckard

bookbub.com/authors/bey-deckard

pettingzoo.co/@Beybey

9 781989 250235

PRAISE FOR THE HEX NEXT DOOR

"If The Ex-Hex and Practical Magic had a sapphic baby, it would be The Hex Next Door. A wickedly charming second chance HFN romance wrapped in a snarky, Cozy Witch package."

 - **Justin Arnold**, Author of *Wicked Little Things*

"Once again, Wilham brings together a collection of unique characters who create a beautiful landscape of representation and individuality. The Hex Next Door is a lovely picture of family being more than just blood, and reminds us that those who truly love us, will always find a way to be there for us."

 - **Christis Christie**, Author of *Ephesus*

"Lou Wilham has created a vibrant, unique and queeralicious world. Where magic is part of the mundane, but the true story lies in the depth of the characters. They are fully fleshed out, relatable and diverse. From houses with personalities to the undead, the world painted by Wiham gives the reader the true feeling that magic is right next door and that life is painted in all the colors of the rainbow."

 - **G.D. Roman**, Author of *Bound Island*

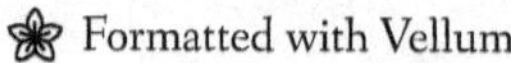 Formatted with Vellum